T0105271

QUESTIONS OF PRECEDENCE

FRANÇOIS MAURIAC

QUESTIONS OF PRECEDENCE

(*Préséances*)

Translated by
GERARD HOPKINS

FARRAR, STRAUS AND GIROUX

NEW YORK

Preface to a New Edition

WHEN this book first appeared in 1921, I had been living away from my native city for fifteen years. Except for members of my family, and some friends, I knew nobody there. My characters, therefore, must not be regarded as portraits of real persons, and my readers should be careful not to put names to caricatures, the very exaggeration of which serves to make them inoffensive.

I have used Bordeaux as my background, but it might just as well be any other commercial city. 'I need not ask whether you come from Marseille'—a woman once said to me, convinced that I had thoroughly enjoyed poking fun at Marseille society. This convinced me that the matter of this small book is of general application.

I think that if I were writing it to-day, I should treat my characters with greater kindness. I have learned to esteem the 'aristocracy of the cork' more highly than any other. It plays, in our modern world, a modest, but clearly defined, part. Since the burning of the Tuileries the hereditary nobility of France has lost its function. But the great wine-cellars of Bordeaux are eternal, and the vintages of my native land have a right to ennoble the families who serve them.

MALAGAR: 17th August, 1928

PART ONE

' . . . I pray not for the world.'
ST JOHN, XVII, 9

I

AUGUSTIN was in the singular position at school of being the only boy who was always top in French Composition, yet always in trouble, because his form-master disliked him. But he was proof against every affront, every unfairness. On those red-letter days in the school calendar when all impositions were cancelled, he would quietly make his way to the place of shame in the corner to which he had a sort of squatter's right, being of those who feel grateful for punishment because it serves to isolate them, who never complain of their lot provided it is different from that of the common herd. He was a guileless youth who would have scorned being 'let off', who could never have borne not to be punished. His very abilities marked him out as a target for the secret rancour of those in authority. More than once he had come to the rescue of the mathematics master when that short-sighted little creature had become hopelessly entangled in a problem: and he corrected the misconstruings of the Latin master with the neatly-tended beard, who shamefacedly concealed under his portfolio a 'crib' of the text through which Augustin found his way with such astounding ease.

At the Sunday theology classes, he was constant in argument, and, armed with invincible logic, drove the chaplain to compromise now with the casuists, now with the Jansenists. He would extricate him from one heresy only to involve him in another, till the poor man resembled a ball in the English version of billiards, always falling into one pocket after another.

To make matters worse, he made tactless use of his victories. He forced his adversary to admit defeat and, so to speak, rubbed his nose in the blunders he had committed. It was clear, from his French essays, that he had not condescended to take a single note, as he was supposed to do, at the lectures which formed part of the Language and Literature course. He affected to admire only certain very ancient, or very modern, poets, and his pastors and masters were faced with the choice either of expelling him or turning a blind eye to his reading. That this was determined by what could be described only as a highly individual taste became abundantly clear in his answer to the question—'Who is your favourite poet? Give reasons for your preference'—in which he devoted a page of extravagant praise to a certain Arthur Rimbaud (who, according to the French master, had probably never existed). To this outrageous behaviour he owed two blissfully happy Sundays of 'detention' thanks to which he was able to avoid a boring walk in the suburbs and a game of football on a patch of mangy grass.

His dirty school uniform, from which all the buttons were missing, his mop of unruly hair and general air of grubbiness, kept us from noticing the fine drawing of his features. In this school for the children of rich families, in which each was valued in terms of the car which came to fetch him after vespers, and I insisted on being called for by a footman and not a maid, Augustin's air of anointed royalty was not of a kind to make any impression on the sons of merchant princes. He was addressed only by his Christian name, and it was general knowledge that some shameful secret hung about his birth. The fact that he was being educated in a luxurious and exclusive establishment, might well have stimulated the curiosity of young and romantic minds. But there was nothing romantic about the sons of Fredy Dupont, John Martineau, Willy

Durand, Percy Larousselle and other heirs-presumptive of the great wine businesses. Their enthusiasms were already limited to the year's handsome profits, to horses and to cars. They thought they were talking about love when they reckoned to the nearest franc the cost of the mistresses of whom they hoped to make a public display when schooldays should be over. In the expectation of that happy moment, they exchanged addresses of those 'places' where—'someone I know has been going for months without catching anything' (for their prudent passions knew nothing of that mettlesome heat which laughs at risks). These young gentlemen affected, in their attitude to Augustin, a contempt which had in it an almost equal dose of jealousy and fear—as well as that physical disgust felt by boys submitted to the discipline of a daily bath—for a squalid little boarder.

I felt that I had, in some sort, to apologize for not being the son of a wine-magnate, but only the nephew of one of those dealers in Trieste timber whose only contact with vintages comes from the wholesale provision of casks. Though conscious of some element of hidden greatness in Augustin, I had, if I were to count for anything with the 'right people' and to maintain my social position, to join in their sniggering. At all costs I must avoid the risk of seeing my aunt's Sunday greetings in the parlour ignored—in spite of our 24 h.p. car—by Madame Willy Durand or Madame John Martineau. These ladies excelled in the art of expressing subtle shades of disdain, goodwill or contempt by means of barely perceptible nods, with or without the accompaniment of a smile (and so graded that one could never be sure of their precise intention, or, should necessity arise, might persuade oneself that perhaps they really had not seen one . . .). Madame John Martineau, for instance, who had been educated at the Sacré Coeur with my aunt, habitually addressed her as 'tu' when they met in the morning, as 'vous' when a third person was present, and affected not to know her at all when they ran across one another in some drawing-room where it was of the first importance not to confuse degrees of social rank. True, as the daughter of a humble lawyer, who had entered the aristocracy of trade only through marriage, she had to step very warily, exaggerate her exclusiveness, and avoid those familiarities which were forgiven in a Madame James Castaingt who was the daughter, wife and mother of Wine, and wholly to the manor born.

Though he was wonderfully indifferent to the *cordon sanitaire* which had been drawn about him, Augustin did, all the same, show a faint liking for me. He, who never looked at anybody, seemed to be quite often conscious of my presence, and never without my being aware of it. I could feel his eyes upon me from a distance. In form he occupied a desk immediately be-hind my own, and, now and again, a feeling of embarrassment made me turn my head. When I did so, I was made the recipient of a fleeting smile which flickered for a moment on the impassive face, only, as quickly, to disappear again. I dreaded his advances, though from them, thank God, I was as a rule pre-served by the constant detentions inflicted upon him by M. Garrouste. Otherwise I should have found it difficult to resist them. There was a warmth in his self-assured air that appealed to something deep within me, with the result that I lived in a condition of perpetual nervousness. 'He is biding his time'— I told myself, and was terrified lest the Sons of the Great Houses might suspect my secret liking for the pariah. Fortu-nately, their globular eyes were incapable of registering such subtleties.

It was just when I was beginning to feel reassured that

Augustin pounced. We seniors were feverishly preparing for the school festivities which always took place on Saint-Joseph's feast day. The programme, that year, was to be something very special, designed to give pleasure to local high-society. The idea was to mount a mock-hunt in the park. The Fredy Duponts had lent their 'drag', their grooms, and a large contingent of domestic attendants. For weeks my family lived in a state of trembling uncertainty. It seemed only too probable that I should be excluded from an occasion in which only those out of the very top drawer would participate. I was the subject of much secret discussion. Young Harry Maucoudinat, the leader of a powerful faction, held the view that the son of a timber-merchant was not entitled to a seat on a 'drag'. My uncle saved what appeared to be a lost cause by putting it about that I was the possessor of a scarlet coat (in fact, this was not ordered until it had been decided that, so dressed, I had the right to mingle on the 'drag' with the Sons, and to share so fully in their glory that I might actually be taken for one of them!).

How well I remember that warm afternoon, the bursting buds on the chestnut trees, the sense of rising sap, and the twittering of sparrows in the early spring sunshine. When, after High Mass, we appeared in our scarlet coats, the boys of the middle and junior forms rushed to the fences which bounded their playgrounds, and gave us an ovation. M. Garrouste maintained that, even in Paris, it would be hard to find a body of gentlemen so well turned-out. Not daring to indulge in play, we strutted like a lot of turkey-cocks clucking with laughter.

It was just then that I became conscious of Augustin's eyes on me, and, though I was determined not to turn my head, turn it I did, and was staggered to see that, for the first time, he was looking in my direction without a smile. The admiration of the world ceased to mean anything to me as soon as I became aware of the pity (unmixed with mockery) on the face of the boy leaning, a little way off, against a tree.

There was a burst from the hunting-horns. I noticed my aunt, all feathers, in a group consisting of the Fredy Duponts, the John Martineaus, the Willy Durands, the James Castaingts, the Harry Maucoudinats and the Percy Larousselles. No one, it is true, was addressing a word to her, but, on the other hand, no one was turning a back, and it was clear that in the eyes of the assembled multitude, all allowance made for certain subtleties of degree, my aunt was being accepted, really accepted, as 'belonging'. We—the scarlet-coated—were standing round the 'drag' at the far end of the Court of Honour, waiting for the moment of our entry. My uncle was sharing in my moment of glory, which was also his. He was wearing a brown suit and beige spats, striking a note of what he supposed to be specifically English elegance. His clean-shaven face was twisted into a grimace as a result of the effort he was making to keep a monocle in his eye. The horses were pawing the ground. A great lout of a groom tried a note on his horn. The organizers had assumed that the 'drag' would arrive empty, but Fredy Dupont, not content with displaying his own splendour, had brought a number of guests with him. 'You'll have to pile in somehow,' he said, but I could see at a glance that, however much we piled in, somebody would have to be sacrificed. My uncle saw it, too. 'Get up quick!'—he whispered. I made a dash for the 'drag' and was just climbing on, when a 'not so much pushing, young man' from the lips of Fredy Dupont made me draw back. 'Somebody will have to give up his place', he added, and I realized that sentence had been passed on me. Having looked us all over, he said that it was I who would have to give way. He was as uncompromising over the smallest details of precedence as the Great King could ever have been at Versailles, and quite unaware of the absurdities of a ritual of which he had, in part, been the creator. Meanwhile, the Sons were looking at us, my uncle and me, with that air of pleasure which people show when exercising their right to impose ostracism. I heard Fredy Dupont say 'Terribly sorry . . . another time . . . ' My uncle, all dignity thrown to the winds, caught at a straw, grovelling. 'Wouldn't there perhaps be room for me on the running-board? . . . ' But no, it was fully occupied by the grooms! The situation was taking on the appearance of a public affront: we had drunk of shame to the dregs. Once again, the horns sounded a flourish, hooves rattled on the cobbles, and there we stood alone, my uncle and I, where the fateful 'drag' had been, among the golden droppings of the horses.

I could see from the look on my uncle's face that the domestic staff was in for a bad time when he got home, and that next morning his typist would be shot to pieces by broadside after broadside of insult and abuse, and would come to me in the evening, after office hours, for the consolation she was by now accustomed to receive. Fearing that the storm might burst over my head, I plunged into the park. The day, by this time, had laid aside its make-believe mask of spring, and it was an icy wind that carried back to me the echoes of the festive day, and those notes on the hunting-horn which had never, previously, held any hint of melancholy, but had merely rasped my nerves with the idiotic vulgarity of their brassy din. Prostrated though I was by the load of my humiliation, and finding my own company unendurable, I was, nevertheless, conscious deep within myself, of an upwelling sense of release and liberation. A leafless alley, where stood an insipid plaster statue of Our Lady from which the sugary colours were slowly flaking, offered me a refuge, and there I hastily gave vent to such tears as I could summon to my eyes. I heard the sound of footsteps, of a voice speaking my Christian name. I recognized it (though it was addressing me now for the first time) and, for the first time, too, I found in myself sufficient strength not to turn my head. But the voice continued:

'Have they, then, dear brother, granted you the favour of your liberty? Shall I really have, no longer, to look on you as the prisoner of deaf-mutes who are blind as well? They are wise to cast you out. In their squalid little minds they dimly realize the temper of your spirit, and know that you could never make common cause with them. . . .'

Secretly I was flattered by this pompous speech, though I had not yet wholly freed myself from the old Adam, and could not resist the temptation to interrupt him with a truly Racinian reply:

'And who, dear lord, has told you I am scorned?'

It gave me great pleasure to hear from Augustin's lips that I belonged with him to the race of intellectuals, and lived in a world far removed from the grooms and chauffeurs at whose hands I had suffered—though rather than admit my exclusion from their company I would have left the town for ever! Here, in Augustin's presence, I wanted it to seem that I attached no importance whatever to the incident of the 'drag', though in my throat I felt that tightening which, as a child, I had experienced when I had been made to swallow a capsule of quinine, and been told that it would soon dissolve. I kept my head turned away while I spoke, because I knew that the sight of Augustin would release tears which were dangerously near the surface. A dampness was rising from the earth. A tiny dead leaf, left over from the winter, quivered at the end of a branch on which the buds had made a premature appearance. The last sounds of the festivities, now near their end—shouts, motor-horns, and engines starting—were dying down. Augustin wrapped me in his cape, and spoke—not of the torments which the day had brought, but of myself, a subject always full of charm for me. He salved my wounded pride. His praise of me was sensitive and tactful.

'How well I remember'—he said; 'the day when this statue of the Virgin was unveiled in the presence of the Cardinal-Archbishop. You had written, and recited, a poem composed for the occasion. The Superior had insisted on its containing a flattering reference to His Eminence. I don't mind telling you that I could never have produced what was needed—but you, somehow, managed to introduce into your Ode to the Virgin, three lines which were both excellent in themselves and cleverly designed to do what had been asked of you:

> . . . *Un grand Pontiffe, ô Reine!*
> *Jette l'auguste éclat de la pourpre romaine*
> *Sur l'humble pompe de nos fleurs!*'

(Admittedly, they weren't bad, but they had cost me dear. The gentlemen of the great Houses, who, in those days, honoured me with their approval, left me in no doubt that they 'had no use for long-haired blighters'—which I took to be directed at me.)

Augustin put his arm in mine, and together we walked away. He begged me not any longer to let myself be distressed by the concerns of trivial vanity, but to take my place solidly in that world of intelligence in which he lived untouchable, and saddened only by a sense of solitude: 'I had determined to give you my love'—he went on: 'and had made up my mind that one single glance from you which, in charity, you would have to spare, should satisfy me.'

He talked on, and I listened. Composure had come back to

me, and I was curious. Not that I had been won over to his lofty ideas, but that it had occurred to me how, by making use of him, I might be able to launch an attack against the Sons of the Great Houses. I knew them too well to expect any gentler treatment at their hands after the way in which they had behaved. All the cock-birds would fall with claw and beak upon the wounded chick! Well, I would stand up to them. Augustin's intelligence and nobility of mind would give me a powerful weapon against them. To the Party of the Sons I would oppose the Party of Genius. The pariah and I would enter into an alliance, and I would use him as a tub-thumper uses the mob. . . . I owe it to myself to say that my sole intention was to get the better of my enemies, to compel them, once again, to accept me. What were those delights of the spirit offered by Augustin when set against the incomparable joy of belonging, for ever and beyond all question to that world which I so longed to inhabit?

II

DINNER, that evening, was a mournful affair. My uncle's blotched dewlaps presented a frightening map of reds and purples. My aunt, with a vague look in her eyes, gave herself up to reckoning the long tale of averted backs, of greetings not returned, of smiles addressed in vain to faces which had become suddenly wooden.

Only my sister, Florence, seemed not to have lost her bearings. It is enough, for descriptive purposes, to say that she belonged to that class of young women whom their elders compare sometimes to china shepherdesses, sometimes to rosebuds. But how false was that seeming fragility! In spite of her patiently acquired English accent; in spite of her fair hair which might so easily have led people to think that she belonged, by right, to the other side of the Channel, her so obviously French —her even eighteenth-century French—full-fleshed figure, as well as the exuberance of her gestures and the comic extravagance of her speech, proved to anyone seeing her for the first time, that she was a true daughter of the South. I had already noticed, behind the innocent blue eyes and the romantic air, the existence of a clear-sighted, calculating little mind. Like all young girls she had but one thought—marriage; but, being madly ambitious, she was secretly resolved to marry only a Fredy Dupont, a John Martineau or a Willy Durand, so that it might be in her power one day to organize a Saint-Bartholomew massacre among her former friends. She thought it high time that *she* should be in a position not to acknowledge

21

the greetings of others. Her dowry had already attracted several aspirants of high lineage, but she valued her native city sufficiently to attach less importance to being the wife of a Morte-mart than of a James Castaingt or a Harry Maucoudinat! She may, or may not, have known that, except locally, those names —Martineau, Dupont, Castaingt—were only vaguely familiar, that the fact of their owners having been enriched at the font with English appellations meant no more than that they were generally regarded as figures of fun: the truth is that her conception of life was that of a gold-fish. The world, for her, was limited to the glass bowl which contained her trivial passions.

I knew that in Florence's eyes my recent adventure in the matter of the 'drag' would assume the proportions of a Waterloo. But I was too familiar with her to be surprised at finding her calmness unperturbed. She refused to believe that the game was lost, and was, doubtless, already engaged in perfecting a plan.

We withdrew to the smoking-room where my aunt could, at last, give free expression to her sense of desolation.

'Even Madame Lartigue turned her back on me, though, Heaven knows, *she* can't exactly be said to "belong". She's about as ordinary as anyone could be. Why, her parents kept a draper's shop on the Place des Célestins, and Lartigue, the pastry-cook in the Cours Delphine is her husband's first cousin (though she doesn't boast of *that*!).'

'You forget'—broke in Florence—'that their son, Gaston, rides at the Horse-Show.'

My aunt's only reply to this was: 'Perfectly true: one must remember that!'—spoken in the tone of one who does not question the mysteries of social precedence.

'Not much chance of that ever happening to *you*'—grunted my uncle, emerging from his state of torpor, and within measurable distance of launching out into the sort of coarse language which, he had been told, was frequently used by smart gentle-men across the Channel.

I replied that it would be still some years before I could hope to put in an appearance at the Horse-Show, but that I had something very much better to suggest which might well serve to restore our shattered fortunes. Three anxious faces were turned to mine. It took them some time to penetrate the deep machiavellism of my strategy. The idea of our not taking our defeat lying down, of our turning on the enemy, at first appeared quite mad to them. It was Florence who first grasped the true inwardness of my projected manoeuvre, and saw that it was worth risking. She had taken the full measure of our fall—being only too knowledgeable in the farmyard habits of the Great Houses not to realize what was in store for us, that, as living victims already riddled with pin-pricks, the more we humbled ourselves, the more surely should we be trodden under foot. Where my uncle was concerned Florence was all-powerful. She, therefore, found no difficulty in persuading him, and in teaching him the part he had to play. It was all a question of spreading, at his club, in his office, and among such people as Hubert, the hair-dresser frequented by the 'smart' people, and Harrison who adorned their teeth with gold fillings, a carefully doctored version, prepared by us, of what had actually occurred. Next day, everyone in town knew that the Sons were jealous of the friendship I had struck up with an infant prodigy the secret of whose princely (perhaps even royal) birth was shrouded in glorious mystery. This Augustin and I were the pride of the school, and the Sons, driven frantic by envy, had satisfied, at our expense, their hatred of intelligence.

I lost no time in obtaining an interview with the Superior, who was also my director of conscience. He was an old man who lived too close to God to understand anything of my complexities. He had reached an age at which he was extremely sensitive and would shed tears on the slightest pretext (a warning sign at seventy-two!). With ill-concealed emotion I spoke to him of Augustin, of the endless punishments inflicted upon that young genius by M. Garrouste. I begged him to do something to put an end to so unworthy a persecution. As soon as he began to show emotion, I knew that I had won.

'You are a noble-minded lad'—he said: 'rest assured that, from now on, your dear Augustin shall be treated according to his merits.'

Though deeply touched at owing his deliverance to me, and sensible of the marks of affection which I showered upon him, Augustin chiefly loved me because I was prepared to follow his advice. It was no longer the Sons who now snubbed me, but I who, as I paced the yard with Augustin, refused to honour them with so much as a glance. Not content with failing to acknowledge two or three proffered greetings, I pushed my daring so far as to refuse the out-stretched hand of Harry Maucoudinat whose fishlike eye showed, for the first time, a glimmer of feeling. Augustin, full to the brim of all the poems of all the poets, applied to him the lines which Victor Hugo had written about a donkey:

> Il avait dans ses yeux noyés d'une vapeur
> Cette stupidité qui peut-être est stupeur.

Not a single blunder in the school essays of those gentlemen but made the rounds of the town, thanks to the diligence of Florence and my uncle. Many of them have now become classics. Not only did I taste the sweet savour of revenge, but found in the company of Augustin a pleasure that was quite new to me. I could at last exchange ideas with someone who was almost as intelligent as myself, and, knowing that, from the very nature of my plan, this state of affairs could not last, that victory would compel me to turn my back upon the marvellous boy, I took, so to speak, double mouthfuls of what he had to offer, and never failed to question him with the air of an adoring neophyte which he found enchanting. I had always been eager to learn the story of his life, which no one knew. But he did not much like talking of the past, and preferred to live in the future. He was a strange creature!

He liked to say that he was free from all bonds, the prisoner of no caste, of no family, and would take his way through the world as someone wholly detached, without blinkers, without traditions, without memories.

On this subject he spoke with tireless eloquence. I listened to him with the assumed timidity of a young bourgeois. Being a subscriber to a doctrinaire journal all the articles in which were richly soused with the sauce of Bonald, Maistre and Le Play, I poured out a deal of not altogether unsubtle criticism of this individualistic and, as I called it, 'romantic' view of life. But Augustin grew indignant when I ventured to compare him with Jean-Jacques. He made, he said, no claim to destroy anything. Society need have no fear of one whose only wish was to remain unknown.

'Can one not live elsewhere than in this tiny peninsula of Europe? Think, my friend, what a savage place the world still is! True to your Latin prejudices, you can never be convinced that beyond the limits of the Empire anything is worth while. For me, on the contrary, that is where the world begins!'

How brightly his eyes shone as he said that! Unable to find words in which to express his ardour, he transmitted it to me through the medium of Baudelaire's *Voyage* and Rimbaud's *Bateau Ivre*, from which two poems, I believe, he drew all of his philosophy.

III

I FOUND my success faintly embarrassing. The squalid
rabble, deeply incensed by the arrogant attitude of the Sons
of the Great Houses, had never, so far, put their feelings
into words, but now our victorious offensive galvanized
them into action. Though an aristocratic sympathizer to the
tips of my fingers, I became a hero to those humble folk whose
very approach turns one's stomach. When the elections came
round, the sitting deputy, Arbanats, just scraped back, but only
after a humiliating second ballot, and it was matter of general
knowledge that he owed this set-back to the fact that his
daughter was the wife of Fredy Dupont, and to the grovelling
efforts he had made to gain access to that world. The examination for the baccalauréat set the coping-stone upon our triumph.
While Augustin and I emerged from the ordeal with honour-
able mentions, the corpses of the Sons lay thick upon the ground,
and the ill-will of the examiners, our accomplices, saw to it
that a full knowledge of their howlers was spread far and wide.
Very soon everybody knew that young Fredy Dupont, having
been set the task of writing, in the person of Virgil, a letter to
the Emperor, had imagined that he would get high marks by
beginning it with the words—'My Dear Augustus'. Harry
Maucoudinat who, by a lucky chance had scraped through on
his written work, was roughly handled at his *viva voce*. Scarlet
in the face, and puffing himself up like a turkey-cock, he said
to the examiner:

'I would have you know, sir, that I am Harry Maucoudinat, junior!'

'And I would have *you* know, sir, that I am examining you in Greek, and give you no marks!'

That sort of thing was quite enough to set the whole town laughing. Such incidents, at a late stage in the campaign, enabled us to sign a glorious armistice at top speed. Advances were made to us by the Sons which, at any other time, would have filled us with heavenly rapture. The Committee of the *London and Westminster Club* let my uncle know in a round-about way that his candidature would be more than welcome, and so dazzled was he that he would then and there have embarked upon a policy of mutual understanding had not Florence strongly opposed any relaxation in an offensive which, she was quite certain, was bound to end in a crushing victory for us, and a marriage for her with one or other of the Sons. Though I was not quite so convinced as she was of so glorious an issue, I backed her up, though I knew in my heart of hearts that the reasons I advanced were not the true ones. I had reached a point at which I could no longer do without Augustin's good opinion. The thought of how he would look when I unmasked my batteries and passed into the enemy's camp, set my cheeks flaming. Though I detest any display of foolish sentimentality, I am compelled to admit that his friendship was becoming more and more precious to me with every day that passed. I was caught in my own trap, and, in spite of myself, had become the prey of the boy who had been my dupe.

It was decided that he should spend the holidays in our villa at Gravette. What chiefly worried my uncle was the problem of Augustin's wardrobe, for he had no evening clothes, and my uncle could not endure the thought of anyone not dressing for dinner.

'How can we be sure'—he grumbled—'that the young ragamuffin will appear even at breakfast in the right clothes?'

'Or that he won't blow his nose with his fingers?'—put in Florence. 'Well, war is war, and we need him badly.'

My aunt objected that we might find it difficult, later on, to get rid of him.

'We'll drop him like a hot brick the moment he's of no further use to us,' said Florence, turning her angelic eyes full upon me. I lowered my own for fear she might see in my face the signs of an emotion which I, no less than she, regarded as fundamentally absurd.

The mystery surrounding Augustin's origins made it necessary for him to stay on at school even in the holidays. Now that he had matriculated he would remain there until the beginning of term, when he would exchange his status as pupil for that of master.

'Just long enough to save a bit of money'—he told me—'and rig myself out, after which I shall clear off.'

'Where shall you go?'

'I don't care, so long as it's away from Europe.'

When I invited him to come to us, he at first flatly refused:

'How could your people stand having a savage with them for so long?'

'But don't you see it would mean that I shouldn't have to be without you, Augustin?'

I could see that these simple words had overcome any objections he could make. Faced by the prospect of so much happiness, he surrendered:

'Summer days with you at the sea . . .' he began.

All resistance was at an end. We made endless plans during

those evening recreation periods which preceded Prize Day, when somewhere a little rain had fallen, and a fresher breeze stirred the leaves already past their glorious prime: when the air was filled with the scent of wood-shavings from the hastily erected platforms, and the smell of red-and-white striped canvas marquees. If I shut my eyes I can still recapture them, mingled with that other smell of tall, sappy grass crushed under our rope-soled shoes. . . .

Gravette lies on the northern side of the inlet which bears its name. For twenty years it has patiently watched the sea eating away the shoreline, and now there is nothing left. At the time of which I am speaking, the waves were already breaking agains the terrace-walls of the villas, all of which belonged to the various 'Great Houses' of the city. The different chatelaines lived in their few square feet of garden, exchanging guarded greetings over the dividing walls. They sat, with their needle-work, facing the sea, which they liked to say they never grew tired of watching, because it was never the same from one moment to another . . . though, in fact, they had eyes only for the coming and going of the boats—known hereabouts as 'pinnaces'—all agog to identify the passengers, and thus be in a position to distribute with strict fairness to each according to rank, greetings, smiles, head-shakes and thin-lipped dis-approval.

On Sundays the excursion trains disgorged their boisterous crowds of trippers. These, however, soon grew discontented, because there was no beach to sit on, and because the villas, drawn up in battle-order, had taken possession of the sea in the interest of the social lights who owned them. I know of people who have spent a whole day at Gravette without so much as catching a glimpse of a crested wave. There is also a forest where those suspected of consumptive tendencies live in chalets which are never disinfected, for the purpose of pinning a label to such ailments as they may be suffering from. By means of a motor-launch Augustin and I could quickly reach the other side of the inlet to where dunes, glittering like hills of rock-salt, border the dark-blue stretches of the ocean and, with their ragged crown of jade-green pines, make a Japanese silhouette against the sky.

I can still see again in memory the arrival of Augustin, in the glare of the midday sun, on our verandah with its furniture from Maple's. Even now I feel a sense of bitter shame to think that my knowledge of the human heart should not have given me warning of what would happen. No sooner had he paid his respects to his host and hostess, with more ease of manner than I had dared hope, Florence got up from her chair, and offered him her hand.

'You are a very old friend, Monsieur, or, rather, more than a friend, for my brother looks on you as a brother, and I find it hard to believe that this house has not always been your home.'

I felt sure that Augustin had never in his life been at such close quarters with a woman as when, taking that small hand in his, he mumbled unintelligible words—nay more, that he had never in the whole course of his miserable existence heard the somewhat low-pitched voice of a young girl speaking words to him that had an almost tender sound. But there, too, I showed myself to be a wretchedly bad psychologist! I should have known our Florence's charming character well enough not to be taken in by her tricks. As it was, I really did believe that, at first sight, she had found him not altogether unpleasing. Washed, combed, and wearing a decent suit which, with perfect simplicity, he had accepted from me as a gift, he made a striking impression. To say that he was 'handsome' would be an understatement, for the dominant look in his face was one of youthful and extreme nobility. There was something for which I can find no other word than 'august' in his air of innocence—an expression at once pure and wide-awake, an odd harmony of intelligence and candour. Surely, for all her sophistication, Florence should have been touched by so much grace? How could that wretched little doll's organ which she called her heart not have sprung into life with a quickened beat . . . or, in default of heart. . . . At luncheon, my horror-stricken uncle and aunt noticed that after the fish-course he did not leave his fork on his plate, that he even went so far as to eat the piece of bread with which he had wiped it, and had stuffed a corner of his napkin into his waistcoat. Florence questioned him about his reading, and, to my amazement, said nothing positively stupid.

That afternoon, as the launch ploughed through the thick water, it was he who talked, she who listened. She sat in the stern, her head all aureoled with light, and her eyes fixed upon him. To the compassion in her look he responded with a hymn of praise.

Merely by living, he declared, we could pay the debt of infinite praise which we owe to the giver of all life. What mattered a past of wretchedness? What mattered the tears shed in secret and confided only to the hard pillows of our schoolboy beds, tears stifled when the shadowy form of the usher on duty emerged from the darkness, entered the flickering circle made by the night-light, then vanished again into the dense shadows of the dormitory, between the twin rows of beds looking like children's graves? . . . What importance had such things compared with the blazing blue above our heads, with the sea on which we three were moving in blissful isolation, with the

mythological gulls swooping about our heads, and the unreal
dunes towards which we were travelling, as to the happy isles?

Much to my surprise, Florence broke in on him with two
lines from *l'Invitation au Voyage*. Augustin was loud in his
praise of her for orchestrating, on a theme of Baudelaire, all
the inexpressible beauty of the day.

By the time we got home, he was intoxicated, dazzled and
enthralled. At table, he spilled his lyrical enthusiasm into the
outraged ears of my uncle and aunt. He poured himself copious
draughts of wine with a gesture which, though there was
nothing in it of vulgarity, betrayed a complete absence of
experience. He spoke only to Florence and me, so exclusively,
indeed, that the master and mistress of the house began to
doubt their own existence, and felt that they were, intellectu-
ally, of no more importance than the decanters. I thought they
seemed appalled by the presence of this young tramp who
picked his teeth with his fingers, mopped his moist, though
noble, forehead with his napkin, and rubbed his plate so clean
with a piece of bread, that when the servant took it from him it
looked so bright and spotless that it might never have been used
at all. Still brooding on the knowledge that they would have
to put up with the visitor for the whole of the holidays, they
went up to their room where, I felt sure, my uncle relieved
his feelings with a fit of shouting the sound of which was
mercifully drowned for us in music. Florence, at the piano,
was completing her careful task of seduction. Though Augustin
was familiar with church-music, he was now, for the first time,
and until late into the night, with his forehead pressed to the
window which framed a moving space of clouds and stars
and waves, being initiated into the sensual magic of Beethoven
and Schumann.

We slept in the same room. He could not bear the thought

of going to bed, nor yet of shutting out the day just past with curtains. When sleep took hold of me, he was still standing before the open window, and, by the glimmering of the night sky, my heavy eyes could see his hair stirring in the breeze.

He was still sleeping when I awoke. He lay there like one utterly exhausted, an angel crushed and prostrate. I went and scratched at Florence's door. She opened it, and I saw that she was already up, wearing a beach-dress with sandals on her bare feet. She asked after our 'Huron', and I, in my turn, enquired whether it was love that had opened to her the gates of Baudelaire. There was something terrifying in her gay burst of laughter. She said that, since we had to put up with the boor, we might as well get what amusement we could out of him, adding that she was by no means averse to experimenting with so odd a flirtation. Though Augustin, she said, would sooner or later wake from his enchantment, and be cast by her into his natural nothingness, she would still be grateful to him.

'Be careful, Florence!'—I warned her: 'this heart is very different from the hearts you play with. You had better beware of the fire that you are kindling, of a love which may well be fierce and terrible!'

That, she replied, would be too good to be true. She wasn't counting on it.

'But I know him, Florence: the poor lad is going to suffer.'

She looked at me so oddly that I blushed. I tried to talk to her in her own language. I knew, I said, that Augustin's sufferings were not important, but that, after all, we needed him. . . . She reassured me. She wouldn't pitch him overboard until he had ceased to be useful.

'You see, I have got to handle him in such a way as to get from him what you have so long wanted.'

Seeing that I failed to catch her meaning, she went into greater detail:

'Don't you see, my dear, that we must make him tell us about that mysterious past of which you are so curious. You can take it from me that he will not leave this house until we know the last word about him.'

This bait she offered in return for being allowed to play as she wished with the young man's heart. At first I felt inclined to put him on his guard, but did not. I was an accomplice in what was being plotted, and agreed to hand over my friend to her in the hope of getting the truth about his melancholy secret. What treachery there can be in silence!

IV

THE state of my aunt's liver was sufficient excuse for a
trip to Vichy with my uncle, who made it clear to me
that he hoped, on his return, to find the house swept
and garnished. Augustin had, once and for all, excluded the
pair of them from his own particular world, and did not even
notice their absence. He seemed to be not even aware of my
melancholy, though at one time it would have aroused his
affectionate concern. All that rose for him from the waves was
the one and only Florence. Nothing mattered to him now but
a young girl, standing with her head leaning slightly towards
him, against a background of dunes and flights of gulls which
filled the seaside sky with snow.

All the same, my friend devoted his mornings to me. At ten
o'clock Florence, regularly splashing about in the water at the
bottom of the terrace, dripping wet and cupping her mouth with
her hands, would call to us to join her. At this invitation, Augustin took to his heels and led me as far as possible from the sea,
into the stifling pine-woods where the sand was so hot that it
burned our feet through our *espadrilles*. In a turmoil of flies
and cicadas he walked, as though made drunk by sunlight and
finding only irritation in my moans. He was dreaming at such
times of lands where an insupportable and atrocious heat would
lay him prostrate and suck all ardour from him. Back from
these expeditions, he would sit sweating at the table, his hair
all tousled and his shirt unbuttoned, as though offering his
young and heaving chest as a target to the blows of that most

evil young woman. And I, at such times, would, in the antique mode, call on Venus who avenges lovers, preying on those perfidious hearts which, strong in coldness, find a pleasure in indifference. I waited for the miracle to happen, hoping to see a Florence suddenly all fire, consenting and without resistance.

I remember well one torrid afternoon when Augustin had fallen asleep on the verandah. My sister was looking at him with so strange a concentration and so vivid an expression of joy, that I took her hand, and said:

'Florence, how strangely you stare at your victim!'

She shrugged her shoulders, and I saw that she was looking beyond the prostrate Augustin at the sea.

'I have seen him!'—she said: 'I have spoken to him!'

Who could it be who had disturbed the shrewd and careful Florence? She continued, now suddenly talkative:

'I was floating on my back, and he shyly swam towards me.'

I put no question, but waited for her to tell me the name of the unknown.

'The water, you know, is his element! When his fishlike face emerges from it, he really looks almost presentable. There is something in his porpoise eyes that almost moves me!'

'Harry Maucoudinat!'—I exclaimed.

'It had never occurred to me that simply my bathing at the same time as he did would have brought him so quickly into my net. . . . According to my calculations, the presence here of the "Huron", and the favours I was showering on him, would merely raise the temperature of our porpoise friend a few degrees. . . . That showed lack of confidence on my part! What your strategy has started, I have brought to a head simply by floating on my back!'

She stretched her two bare arms behind her head, offering her bosom to the light, as though she were resting upon outspread wings. At her feet the sacrificial victim was sleeping like one dead.

She gave me a fuller account of the advances made by the 'Son' who, at first, had intended only to have a game with her. But, quicker-witted than his younger brother (whose proffered hand I had refused to take), the elder of the Maucoudinat brood, knew perfectly well that even a business-man, if he is only twenty-four, stands little chance of bluffing a sea-sprite when she sweeps back her wanton curls with a dripping forearm.

'What a catch, Florence!'

She smiled at seeing me thus dazzled. I had forgotten the existence of the sleeper, the sound of whose deep and gentle breathing, when we two momentarily fell silent, filled the verandah.

'Ah, Florence, this heir to a great name has come to you like a Dauphin, who, prepared to submit to a political marriage and suddenly confronted by his yet unknown princess, recognizes in her the woman of his dreams!'

She shook her head, and her laughter sounded strident.

'Oh!'—she said—'all the porpoise saw was a young woman with a settlement of one hundred thousand francs!'

I remember that this blasphemy had been uttered in the very presence of an incarnation of great love. With my finger to my lips, I warned her to keep silent, gesturing with my head towards the unhappy youth.

'Fom now on you will have no further need of him. I'll manage matters so that he can leave us without too much heartbreak. Now that you are happy, you must be kind.'

Once more the hard look came into her face, and she sketched denial with her hand:

'I am not happy, since I am not in love. Do you think I haven't envied that poor devil there? He loves me and needs no pity. Oh, don't worry!—I shall have more than my fill of love—but first I must have assurance that I am no longer humiliated!'

I broke in on her with sugary words: 'And that you, too, can, in your turn, humiliate?'

'I've got what I was after! It will be time enough later to worry about what you call love!'

'But, Florence, do you really think that love will come in answer to your call? Look well at that boy sleeping there. To few of us is it granted to know more than once that we are loved. Look well upon those full, half-opened lips, those lashes and that hair, because a night may come when you may clutch your head between clenched fists, seeking to conjure up a phantom from the past, and, with a cry to summon him . . .'

These things I said believing them to be no more than a patch of literary purple: but I know now how much truth there was in them. With drooping head she listened, and did not try to laugh away what I had told her. It may be that for one fleeting moment her heart was freed from its habitual load of trickery, calculation and trivial vanity. Then, once again those infinitely petty preoccupations flowed back upon it, and I heard her sneering laugh. But I did persuade her to leave to me the task of dismissing my friend, though she insisted that I should do nothing until he had confided to us the secret of his life. Must I confess that she found no difficulty in extracting that promise from me?

Just then, Augustin heaved a deep sigh, opened his eyes, and smiled at us.

Florence said:

'We were looking at you while you slept.'

My friend replied:

'That makes me very uncomfortable: there are so many things to be read in a sleeping face!'

Her next words had in them a note of gentle reproach:

'Even in sleep you guard your secrets well. There is one whole part of yourself which you conceal from us, from us who love you.'

He got to his feet, and, when he spoke, his voice was harsh.

'Do you think you have the right to twist words from their true sense? When you say "love" have you the slightest idea what that means?'

I had moved a little way off, but not so far as to prevent me from hearing Florence say with terrifying sweetness.

'Yes, Augustin, I know what *to love* means.'

The prudent pinnaces had turned, making for harbour. A squadron of heavy clouds was assembling in the west, where now the Atlantic was noisily assailing the sandy shore. I remember Augustin's livid face, the rather plebeian gesture with which he wiped his damp forehead with the back of his hand. She, however, with thoughts only for her wretched trickery, went on:

'Are you never going to tell me what you were like as a child? I feel I have some claim to know about your past. Will you not open the door that I may no longer feel a stranger?'

I saw a flicker of suspicion in his eyes, as though he were faintly conscious of something too pressing in her purpose, something discordant in the tremolo to which she had treated him. But he did no more than make a gesture of refusal, standing silent, with his face pressed to the streaming windowpane.

V

Be back twelfth for betrothal ceremony—Florence. This telegram made my aunt do something which must, I think, be unique in the annals of her life. She interrupted her cure. Though she would gladly have sacrificed the entire human race on the altar of her liver, she stoically faced a night in a sleeper and charmed her insomnia with such happy dreams that the time seemed short. From the upper bunk, my uncle called down to her:

'D'you think it's Willy Durand's eldest boy?'

My aunt screamed back through the noise of the wheels:

'What does it matter which it is, so long as it's one of the Sons!'

They knew Florence too well to doubt for a moment the reality of her triumph, and what, after all, did the name matter? The Sons of the Great Houses are, to some extent, interchangeable—all correct (dressed by the same tailor), all fond of sport, all leaving their offices each afternoon at five, and all exempt from the common laws of civility, in a position to acknowledge or to snub others, as they, the incorruptible dispensers of social ostracism may decide. . . . As some people sing excerpts from operas to themselves, so did my aunt recite, to the beat of the wheels, the litany of her visiting-list, awarding 'marks' with cogitated accuracy, already passing sentence of death on her most intimate friend, establishing a Black Book of her relations, dividing those whom, at a pinch she *could* invite to the nuptial Mass from those to whom it would perhaps be wiser to send

40

a bald announcement of the event, which they could read as being in the nature of a definitive farewell: poor Adila, for instance, that old cousin whom she could not, with the best will in the world, impose upon the family of her niece's husband-to-be. Thus brooding, my aunt carefully erased from her list, with a sigh, as though death had removed her, that same Adila who had been present at her own wedding.

On the station platform at Gravette my uncle and aunt sniffed, as it were, an armistice in the very air, and read it in the smile of one of the Fredy Duponts—their future nephew perhaps—in any case one of Florence's eventual allies (for the Sons, like Kings, are all of the same blood, and refer to one another, among themselves, as 'my cousin'). We were there to meet the travellers. '*Really!*' they said ecstatically: 'a Harry Maucoudinat!'—for though in the 'great world' as in Heaven, each is perfect in his own way, there is, in that perfection, a hierarchic pattern beyond the understanding of simple mortals, though fully comprehensible to the initiated. A Harry Maucoudinat is one degree higher than a Willy Durand or a Percy Larousselle, though to explain why would involve one in enough subtleties to send one mad! On the way to the house, already in receipt of recognitions for which they had never dared to hope (including a wave of the hand from old James Castaingt!) my uncle and aunt, in the parts of distinguished elders, sang their '*nunc dimittis*'.

At table, the presence of Augustin disturbed their happiness. He scarcely greeted them. In his stained and grubby suit, with his dirty cuffs and his unbrushed hair, he still managed to assert himself as a reigning king at the far end of the table, and I remembered how, in his letter to the Queen of Sweden, Pascal gives the name of 'sovereigns' to those who have reached a high degree of knowledge. No doubt about it, he could feel the rising storm, and looked at Florence with a more than usually clear-sighted eye; but he surrounded himself in a cloud not wishing any longer to see reality. For some short while he had been helping himself to live the life of a sleep-walker by taking rather too much wine and spirits. My uncle and my aunt watched him fill and empty his glass, wipe his mouth with the old plebeian gesture, and then sit with his elbows on the table, as though he were at an inn. My uncle went purple in the face. Florence said something in a low voice which calmed him. The meal ended in silence. Only Augustin seemed to be in no way concerned. He was really and truly somewhere else.

When Florence brought my coffee to the verandah, she gave me to understand, though scarcely moving her lips, that the official betrothal ceremony was fixed for the next day. We had only that afternoon, therefore, in which to complete our designs upon the 'Huron'. Then, in her natural voice, she suggested an expedition to the further side of the inlet, there to drink white wine and eat shellfish at an inn famous for those things. Augustin's face lit up. Did he know that on this trip in the bright sunlight, seated beside Florence, he would taste of happiness for the last time? The sleeping wavelets were breaking against the terrace wall with a sound like that of tearing silk. Not a breath of wind disturbed the heat which lay, with heavy solidity, upon the earth and sea. The sails of the little yachts hung motionless. From the next-door villa came the sound of patient scales punctuated by the maddening beat of a metronome. I waited, with my nerves on edge, for the precise moment when the little girl would inevitably strike the wrong note. My uncle in his wicker chair began to snore. At the far end of the garden we could hear the engine of the launch which Augustin was bringing round to the steps. He helped Florence in, and we started. She was wearing a white linen skirt and an open-work blouse which revealed the details of her youthful breast, the flesh showing like the pieces of a jig-saw puzzle between the multiple diamond-shaped patches of embroidery. She had decided that Augustin should sit beside her in the narrow stern. The purr of the engine as we drove through the oily water was as strident as the scraping of cicadas. Florence let her bare arm trail over the side, and then, with a childish gesture, laid it to Augustin's lips.

'See how salt it tastes'—she said.

I think that he was already so drunk that nothing could have added to his drunkenness. Without the slightest sign of distress, he kept his mouth upon the captive, sun-tanned arm, as though it were a bunch of grapes. Then, before Florence could snatch it away, he bit savagely into the flesh. Anger drove the colour from her cheeks for a second, but she hid her temper behind a feigned show of indulgence and gave him a thin-lipped smile, displaying with a look of reproach, the marks of his teeth. He replied that they would have vanished before nightfall, and added:

'I only wish I could have marked you for all eternity.'

I had never before heard that hoarse voice, nor seen those cruel eyes, that puckered forehead and criminal expression. Eastwards a dark wall of mist was staining the blue. Thousands of pines must be flaming to high heaven over there. A smell of burning increased my fear of Augustin, of the fierce and unleashed beast which had suddenly been revealed to me. At last the land drew near. We could hear the nasal scraping of a gramophone. The launch ran up on to the sand, and Florence uttered a sigh.

We sat at a table under a scanty trellis. Disdaining the sea-fresh little oysters for which Gravette is famous, Augustin, with–

out any help from us, emptied a whole bottle of heavy white wine. The American cloth surface was indelibly marked by the circular stains of glasses. In a mood of desperate daring, Florence began to drive her saps forward which, she hoped, would, in the long run, undermine the young man's defences. She, no more than I, could any longer doubt that he knew what was in store. Because of the wine, his great eyes looked serene. It was as though they could read, through the miserable murk of our gerrymandering, right into our hearts. He had undone the collar of his shirt, and the shadow of leaves played on his bare chest. With one elbow on the table, and his hand buried in the tangle of his hair, he watched our slow coming to the point in undisturbed tranquillity. So deeply ashamed did I feel at the thought that he knew everything about my imbecile manoeuvring, that I tried to express in a look all, that as I now realized, I had felt for him. That first flooding-in of tenderness, in which neither self-interest nor hot blood had played a part, had revealed to me the existence in myself of virgin regions, of perspectives, as yet unsuspected, of candour and of sacrifice. . . . How hot it was! Florence, like one who knows the battle has been untimely joined, plunged willy-nilly forward. Then, as though words had failed her, sat silent. At last he began to speak:

'What right have I to refuse to tell the story you so long to hear now that, thinking that you have bamboozled me, you have laid on me a weight of bitter knowledge? Because of what you have done, I am armoured in distrust, and shall be so until I die. There is nothing hid from me of your hateful trickery, and it has taught me the nature of a woman's wiles. Women are not inventive: they always weave the same old web. That revelation, now mine for ever, I owe to you.'

Thrown now completely off her balance, Florence tried to

laugh: but the laugh sounded hollow. With a wicked glint in his eye, he continued:

'I could have punished you by forcing you to carry through your lesson to the very end, and, had I wished it, these arms, these two hands, would have . . .'

I broke in on him, and he outfaced me with a sneer: but Florence intervened:

'Don't you see that he is only joking, that the heat has set his nerves on edge, that he is prepared to buy our absolution with a story that is well worth the telling?'

'My story . . . my story . . .'—he said, in a voice that had suddenly gone dreamy: 'do you think that I have often told it, even to myself? For years I have not ventured to tread the pathways of my past, so that now, if I do so, I cannot tell what horrors may not be revealed in me. I have to grope my way through the shadowed places of my childhood. . . . Who knows? . . . Perhaps even you, Florence, will be forced to weep, and that, maybe, is all my destiny is good for, to set a spring of tears gushing from the rocky desolation of your heart. . . .'

Nothing could have been more unexpected than this sudden change of tone—after such fury, this pure note of tenderness, as, when a storm has passed, one hears the rain-drops falling one by one upon the leaves, bringing the sweet sense of deliverance and pardon. We were careful not to interrupt this prelude, but, with our eyes upon his lips, waited like children for the promised tale. Even Florence's expression showed more than a merely greedy curiosity. At first it came to me that she was utterly unlike her usual self. But then I thought that on the contrary, perhaps, this was her true face, as it might have been before the world had laid upon it a succession of strange masks—the face which God had made and modelled with so much love.

VI

'WHEN I plunge into the thick darkness of the years now gone'—Augustin began—'I feel caught in a tangle of roots and branches. I no longer understand the meaning of "forgetting": everything is there, down to the smell of gas and oil-cloth on the stairs, the halo made on the ceiling by the lamp brought in by Annette, and the way in which the cornice broke it, all the patterns of all the wall-papers in the different rooms, my toys, and the rocking-horse with one hoof missing, the hollow in the floor of the linen-cupboard which held a treasure-trove of lost pins and needles, the way in which the light changed with the time of day or the nature of the seasons, the rustling sound made by the morning paper when the concierge pushed it under the door. Forgetfulness is nothing but a lazy refusal to isolate each of these million sounds and smells and colours. What makes a poet is, surely, the love of these things, a desperate search for the tiny ray of sunshine which used to flicker on the floor of a child's bedroom. The difficulty I find in satisfying your impatient wish to revel in my paltry secrets, is due, therefore, not to my remembering nothing, but to my remembering everything. As I look into my past, I see it as a dense green forest. Which leaf of all the leaves shall I pick, which flower of all the flowers? Which voice, out of a confusion of voices, shall I now recall, and how, above all, distinguish the succession of those voices in time? That world in my eyes and in God's, shows as a vast expanse of breaking wave-crests in the dimen-

46

sion of eternity. Was I five, or ten, years old when I used to stand for hours in front of the looking-glass, misting it with my breath, pressing my face to it, tracing with my fingers the reflected shape, amazed at the thought that I really existed, that I was a human being with a face that was the replica of no other face, with a shape that was unique, different from every other similar shape in all the world?

'I see myself leaning on my elbow at the window of a vast living-room (to me, at least, it seemed vast) where my father sits working, leaning out over a squalid suburban street filled with the rattle and the banging of trams. Instinctively I withdraw my head when the sound of tramping in the street tells me of a hoard of men and women disgorged, or absorbed, by the nearby factory. Machinery groans and whines. Pinker than the obelisk, the chimneys reach so high that they stain even the clear spring heaven. I am filled with hatred, not only of the houses opposite, but of the little patches of workmen's gardens with their skimpy tunnels shorn of leaves which look so grotesque in the livid light of winter, of the shanties in which mysterious ragpickers lived, of whom Annette used to tell me tales which terrified me in childhood. Maybe I did not know, though now I do, that my heart began to beat with a quieter rhythm only when the shutters had been closed and the curtains drawn, when all the sounds from outside were muted, and the lamp burned in its accustomed place, knowing nothing of dawn or dusk, its steady light undimmed by smoky fumes. Radiance glowed in its incandescent mantle, and the scratching of my father's pen gave me the measure of the silence. On the table stood a great pile of books, seeming to weigh it down, some wide open in lively converse with him, others shut, but bristling with markers—waiting, as it were, to be called upon, and ready to disburse the offering of their silent wisdom.

How serene were those evening hours of labour, and how all I wished of them was that they should bring forgetfulness of bedtime! The toys in the shadowed corners were miracles of silence, and my hands had early learned the secret of how to turn the pages of a book by Grandville, without making a sound. With unmoving lips I held endless colloquies with myself, with one or other of my playthings, or with the man on the chimneypiece who sat, elbow on knee and fist to jaw, who looked to me so infinitely unhappy, whose name, though I did not know it then, was *Le Penseur*. Serenity rippled in the great folds of the brown window-curtains, filling them with darkness and reflected light. Like the smell that meets one on the edge of a forest, it came out at me from the disordered piles of books which reached from floor to ceiling, those most familiar within reach of my hand under the lamp, others inaccessible, lost on remote, mysterious heights where all was dust and darkness.

'I can still hear the sound of the penholder dropping on the table. My father pushes aside with his two hands the circle of manuscripts and books. He stretches his bent body and raises his head. As far back as I can remember, I see his face as that of an old man. There is nothing in it of the peace of the late hours and the well-loved objects. He sits with his hands clasped across his bald forehead. At the corners of his mouth are two deep, bitter folds. I think of him always as clean-shaven, though there was a time when he let his beard and moustache grow, but because they were sparse and untidy, cut them off again. When that anguished face rose above the wall of books and manuscripts, all sense of tranquillity vanished from the room. No sooner had his eyes rested on me than I lost all wish to avoid passing the night in sleep. On the contrary, I hurriedly leaned forward to receive his good-night kiss. Not that my father was severe, nor even lacking in tenderness. No, it was just that, so far as a child can be sensible of so strange a misery, I felt, confronted by it, something like fear, like shame—like anguish.

'One evening, when I got back from the school where he had recently placed me, I asked him why one of the boys had pointed at me, saying to his friends: "See that chap? he's a . . . . ." ' '

The word for which Florence and I were so hungrily waiting, stayed for a moment on Augustin's lips, but he did not speak it. Instead, he lapsed into silence, and we were afraid that he would say no more. I signed to Florence to wait until, of his own accord, he should go on with the story. The blaze of the afternoon had kept all saunterers from the shore. Through the green blinds of the inn fumes of absinthe were drifting, and overpowered the smell of the sea. We could hear the sharp impact of billiard-balls, and a sleepy voice calling the score. Above the whisper of the tired waves which sounded like a sleeper's breathing, we could hear the scraping of cicadas. Augustin was no longer even bothering to chase away the tormenting wasps, and, when he started to speak again, it was as though he had forgotten our presence, and, for his own wry pleasure only, was tearing his face and hands upon the branches of the thickset years.

'After that'—he said—'I did not go back to school. Madame Etinger undertook my education. Madame Etinger! . . . Madame Etinger! I can see you still. You rise before me as a figure of both wretchedness and glory. You were proud in your memories of wealth and luxury, and you wore your poverty like a crown. One winter evening, I recall, your feet were bare inside your broken shoes. Your fingers, blue with cold, were sticking through your thread gloves, and I took them between my two hands to warm them. All the time you

gave me my lesson you were slowly eating hot roast chestnuts
—perhaps the only meal of your day. How grey and worn you
looked, and how you loved to fill my dreamy childhood with
stories of Monsieur Oscar Etinger who, when business of importance kept him in Amsterdam or London, sent you every
day an orchid or a rose. This he did, even on the night when,
after changing into full evening-dress at the Savoy Hotel, he
swallowed poison. Annette hated you because you carried off
the leavings of our table, and, when I spoke of you with pity,
said: "If she's starving, why doesn't she take a place as a cook?"
You were for ever changing your lodgings because of dunning
tradesmen, and because your daughter, Eva, could not bear to
eat anything but hot-house fruit, game and every sort of
delicacy. Wandering from district to district, pursued by a
greedy pack of creditors, you resolutely refused to admit that
anything was too expensive for your darling whose close-
cropped hair exaggerated the thinness of a sickly face in which
the eyes burned with love and sadness. She used to come sometimes on Sunday. She adored children and would have liked
to have a little brother like me. She did not realize that I
was already a big boy, and would take me on her lap, rocking
me in the fragrant odour of her arms, and hugging me to
sleep.

  'My father thought highly enough of Madame Etinger to
entrust me to her, but he never felt at ease with her perhaps
because she brooded over him with an air of watchful compassion, and prided herself on a loyalty which was never afraid of
being importunate. To-day I can see what then was hidden
from me. By the very force of her attachment, Madame
Etinger compelled my father to remember others who had
been less faithful. Her mere presence was a yardstick by which
to reckon the number of those defections which, at one period

of his life, had left him prostrate. It did not seem to occur to Madame Etinger that she was deserving of praise for not having made a gesture of denial like the others.'

Florence could no longer contain herself:

'But what had your father done?'

Augustin did not answer: I am not even sure that he heard the question. Assailed by too many pictures from the past, all emerging into memory at one and the same time, he stopped like a traveller who has reached a place where many ways converge, and hesitates which to take. For a moment he wandered from the Etinger road, and retraced his steps.

'Not all my evenings,' he said, 'were suited to meditation. Twice a week, on the stroke of eight, the sound of footsteps at the bottom of the stairs, of laughter outside the front-door, warned me of the enemy's approach. The bell rang, and I took refuge in the kitchen, where Annette was busy preparing glasses of grog, and setting out bottles of beer on a tray. The invaders surged into my father's room, and only when they had been swallowed up did I venture into the hall. The gas there was turned low, and set the shadows cast by shabby soft felt hats, by inverness-capes, mackintoshes, raglans and cloaks, flickering on the walls. Dripping umbrellas brought the severity of the night into the flat. The clamour of voices frightened me. Sometimes there would be a silence in which only my father's would be audible. Then there would come an interruption, and the confused rumble of words would begin again. Gradually the smell of tobacco began to filter through the cracks of the door. Into one room after another it drifted, and I knew that in the morning it would be hanging in the folds of my chintz curtains. Then I would open the door for Annette and her loaded tray. I could see bearded figures moving to and fro in a thick fog of smoke, while *Le Penseur*, bowed under the heavy hand of some invisible conqueror, looked down upon the company from his high perch.

'There was a picture of him on the purple cover of a magazine which this group of men, under the inspiration of my father, filled with pages of prose which, I had decided once and for all, held no interest for me. The reason I gave myself was the absence of illustrations and stories, though, after all these years, I realize that my indifference was dictated by some obscure prejudice which, in those days, prevented me from even wanting to know how my father's mind was working. The fact of the matter is that I was frightened of that sad thinker wrestling with a feeling of nostalgia for the chains he had thrown off.

'One afternoon in June, Madame Etinger took me into a church, telling me to sit quietly on a chair and wait for her. I saw her make her genuflexion in the Choir, and then move to the right and vanish. The gloomy surroundings were unfamiliar to me, but, from the very first moment, I found the fragrance sweet, and sweet the cellar-like coolness. The shadows of darting swifts streaked the stained-glass windows. I was completely alone. The noises of the tumultuous suburb broke in waves against this island of silence. I made myself as small as possible, and dared not move. I did not know that my father had cast off the yoke of the Master of this house, after serving Him for many years in books which he was now engaged in refuting. He had been a lecturer at the Catholic Institute of N . . . , but a thesis on the Symbolism of Dogmas had led to his resignation. He had abandoned his home. Somewhere I have grown-up brothers and a sister, but I have never seen them. My mother, a Polish student, never lost her faith, and died slowly of his sin, as of a cancer. . . .'

Once again Augustin stopped speaking. The gleam in

Florence's eyes, and my realization that she was not disappointed, came as a surprise. I had convinced myself that my friend was the child of a married priest—of some such character as is to be found in the pages of Barbey d'Aurevilly or Villiers de l'Isle Adam—and thought this story of his very mediocre stuff. But now it seemed that Florence had received from Augustin, over and above this sorry secret, another sort of revelation of which I was not worthy.

My friend's voice once more took up the tale.

'From whom had I learned all this? I am not certain that it ever entered into my secret colloquies. The only thing of which I am sure is that from the first moment of my dawning intelligence I knew it. No matter how far back my eyes range over the vanished years, I was obscurely conscious of the hostility of Somebody, of the weight of a heavy hand on us. But what I chiefly remember is that the cries of my dying mother reached me through the misty half-light of my third year. . . . Though I might bury my small face in Annette's apron, those vociferations of despair were louder than my sobs. They pursued me into the furthest corner of the kitchen, and even into the concierge's lodge whither Annette had carried me in her arms.

'On that straw chair in a slum church, with my eyes fixed upon the red sanctuary-lamp which seemed to me to be a living thing, I seemed to be hearing those cries still, and would have run away had not Madame Etinger returned with a young priest who eyed me curiously. "You understand, don't you, that nothing must be done behind his father's back?"—he said: "we are very anxious not to have any trouble." Oh! what joy it was for me to be back in the blinding light of the street, in the heat that was threaded through with the cries of children and the twittering of birds! I felt reassured by the life all round me. Madame Etinger must have noticed the misery in my face, for she pushed open the door of a confectioner's shop which set a bell tinkling, and I forgot everything else in the delicious uncertainty of having to choose from the many little cakes on the shelves in front of me. But when, that evening, on the balcony, I leaned out over the summer noises of the street at the hour when the human flood moves more slowly because hearts are heavy and intertwined like branches, thickening with their love the current flowing between the constricting sidewalks, I knew that my memory of that day would never sleep. I had been taken by the shoulders and pushed into the very centre of the kingdom of anguish, to the heart of the rock where my father stood chained and bleeding, for, turning from the window, I saw him under the lamp, his elbow on his knee and his chin on his clenched hand, like that *Penseur* who held sway over his life. Someone I did not know was talking to him in a rather loud voice (no doubt the editor of the magazine). His eyes were bloodshot and I was shocked by his tone. His voice was raised, and I tried to follow what he was saying. They were discussing the contents of the last number. The unknown was blaming my father for having revived old quarrels: "The fight is won"—he was saying—"science has conquered. By going back over our arguments, you show, it seems to me, that you doubt their strength. . . . You do too much honour to our old enemy by galvanizing the corpse."

'The man expressed himself with the ease of a professional schoolmaster. His interlocutor, on the other hand, stumbled over his words. It was as though he were being driven forward by some tumultuous train of thought which made clear speaking difficult. He mentioned the names of men who had been "converted", expressed doubt as to whether any discovery made in the laboratory or established by the instrument of exegesis could ever be sufficiently decisive against an hypothesis so consoling, or to make men accept the sudden disenchantment of an awakening in the deaf and blind dominance of Matter. The unknown laughed and slapped his thigh with the flat of his hand. But what I most remember is the sudden gloom with which he answered:

' "It's easy enough to see how evil is the power concealed in the formularies of our ancient foe. Ah! my poor friend, it is not for nothing that she brought you up upon her knee, that she swaddled you, dandled you, nourished you. You have amassed in laboured articles reasons for not believing: but you, yourself, are unconvinced by them. The tinkle of an angelus bell, the sound of a chant, these things have more power over your heart than any reasoning has over your mind. . . . The guilty son may invent reasons for hating the mother he has abandoned: that does not alter the fact that she is still his mother. Even though she has cursed him, he cannot live in separation from her."

'I could see in the lamp-light the sweat upon my father's head. Like a sleepwalker he rose to his feet and opened the door. "Go away!" he said, "go away!" while the visitor offered clumsy apologies. To these my father made no answer, but pushed the offender before him to the staircase. Then I heard him shoot the bolt of the front-door. The incident was so quickly over that he was back at his table before I had had time to take refuge on the balcony. He sat there very stiff and straight, and so motionless that I was frightened. The lamp revealed only his two unmoving hands, the lower part of his face, and the lips which were not still, though no words came from them. That brief space of time is still for me a living reality. I vividly remember the whole scene. From the maw of the Métro-station a last black mouthful was spewed on to the pavement: in the seven dining-rooms of a new block, seven ceiling-lights, one above the other, shone through seven identical bow-windows. The dust and smoke of the suburb broke up the diminishing light. My eyes, as always at this hour, sought the first evening star. At last my father took his hat and went out: it was his unfailing habit to walk for fifteen minutes before dinner. I saw his stooping figure in flight along the street. He was the passer-by who talks to himself, gesticulates and is stared at. Seizing the chance of his absence, I slipped back into the room, and looked at the bundles of manuscript lying on his table. Their titles caught my eye: *Fausses interprétations messianiques:—Les origines de la confession:—Psychologies des témoins de la résurrection: théorie de la fraude pieuse.*

'I stood there like a child, looking, for the first time, at the sea. Great shores lay open to the eyes of my mind, and I saw the black, ill-defined lines of seaweed left by the receding tide.

'I heard the familiar sound of Madame Etinger's ring at the door bell. Her daughter was with her, and I remembered that this was "their day" (a series of friends invited them to dinner in turn). No sooner had Eva come in, than, at a sign from her mother, she gave me a small book which she begged me not to let my father see. With earnest intensity, she told me to read it, to learn it by heart, for love of her. I opened the hideous little school-manual with a feeling of curiosity. It contained a number of questions printed in italics, followed by didactic answers. Solemnly and, as it were, *ex cathedra*, Madame Etinger declared that it was my right and my duty to study, unknown to my father, the wisdom it contained. She quoted Somebody as having said that we must love Him more than father or mother. The volume vanished into my pocket when I heard my father's key in the lock, but even at that early age I was skilled in keeping my face from betraying anything. Already, silence was, for me, a sure citadel from which the combined efforts of mother and daughter could not dislodge me. In the course of the meal, my father learned, without apparent interest, that Monsieur Etinger had never allowed his wife to wear the same ball-dress twice, and that he had left her, until the last moment, in ignorance of their imminent catastrophe. On the very eve of that final journey to London from which he intended not to return, he had given a large dinner-party at which, she remembered, there had been caviare, quails and other exotic delicacies. These happy reminiscences occupied her until the meal was over. Eva and I were on the balcony. I could only just make out her face (its extreme delicacy gave it a ravaged look). She doled out, rather affectedly, all the things she had been told about the stars, and about the celestial clock which could not work unless wound up by a celestial clock-maker. That sort of "proof", you know, does not have much of an effect on me. How much more preferable should I have found some unreserve on her part, a sweet confiding, any kind of talk indicative of weakness! My heart felt full to bursting in the stifling darkness while I waited for some sign from her which might have loosed its feeling of constriction. If only she had kept silent she might have freed those confidences for which I so hotly longed to find an outlet. But she spoke with the hesitating uncertainty of a child when it gets confused in the telling of a fairy-tale. She marshalled her arguments in the strict order enjoined upon her by her mother and her director. They were too heavy for her unskilful arms to deal with. She lifted them, and flung them in my face, but, perhaps because I was so small, they failed to reach their target. In any case, how pointless it all was! Why make such an effort to prove to me the existence of a Being whose hostility, lying heavy upon us, furnished sufficient evidence of that formidable and unappeasable presence?'

When Augustin paused for breath I pointed out to Florence a mass of storm-clouds gathering in the west, and said that we had better be thinking about getting back. She seemed scarcely to hear me, to be loitering still upon those roads along which, at Augustin's behest we had been moving towards an earlier day that was not our own. As in a dream, we had found ourselves in rooms unknown to us, smiling at faces which, in real life, we should not have recognized. Florence was lost in the byeways of a past which belonged to this strange and melancholy youth. Only the stubborn silence of my friend brought her to her feet. The tide being high, I carried her to the launch in my arms. Augustin had no eyes for us or for the things about us. When the rain started, we tried, but in vain, to make him share with us the shelter of the awning. Until we reached Gravette he sat motionless and bare-headed in a downpour in which sky and sea seem all confounded.

My uncle and my aunt were on the look-out for our return, and flung themselves on Florence with affectionate concern. What a time to risk 'catching a cold!' While a change of under-clothing was warming in front of the fire, they dabbed at her with their handkerchiefs, taking as much care of her as they would have done of a prize filly entered at the Horse-Show. On her they had placed all their hopes. How young my uncle seemed in his summer suit, how brisk and self-assertive. The very air of the villa had a gaiety, an unexpected lightness. How shall I describe the sudden solemnity on the rough faces of the servants? Each one of them felt as though moved up a peg in the estimation of the world. The whole house knew of the greatness now in store for it. On a silver salver in the hall lay the most magnificent collection possible of visiting-cards—all with their corners turned down—not flung casually, but, like little cakes, set out in a row, because my uncle could not bear to think that any should be concealed—what a gleaming galaxy of names upon the metal surface: James Castaingt, Willy Durand, John Martineau, Fredy Dupont, Percy Larousselle, Bertie Dupont-Gunther!

We went into dinner without waiting for Augustin who had not come down.

'By this time to-morrow your fate, my dear, will be officially sealed'—said my uncle.

What ought he to wear for the ceremony?—a short jacket or a tail-coat?—the latter would be the regulation uniform, but what was the right thing at the seaside? From Larousse he learned that nothing was formally laid down for such an unusual circumstance. My aunt, who found the whole discussion thrilling, shrugged her shoulders when my uncle summed up, though not too bluntly, the talks he had had with the lawyers. I gathered that the bridegroom's contribution would turn out to be rather less than middling, but to this she replied that certain names are worth their weight in gold, since their magic syllables throw wide open the doors of houses otherwise inaccessible. She, too, would now be in a position to pick and choose, to interpret the law—as Madame Fredy Dupont put it —the mystical dogma of that world, when she gathered her chosen women friends about her. She augured from Florence's lack of appetite that the future grandeur of a great position was already lying heavy on her niece's not very powerful shoulders, and drew the flattering conclusion that it would be for her to deputize. When we returned to the verandah, conversation lapsed, perhaps because the beating of the rain against the windows made it necessary for us to raise our voices. All of a sudden the electricity failed. We saw the heavens opened and fire descending which, for a brief instant, lit up our rapt faces. In that rapid glare when lightning revealed the world, I thought

I saw, at the bottom of the garden, upright by the parapet and looking out to sea, Augustin without an overcoat, his hair blowing in the wind. Then the darkness closed in. A second flash tore it wide open again, but this time there was no familiar figure leaning out above the waves. My uncle and my aunt retired before their usual time, like children who want to make the morning come more quickly. Florence and I followed them. At the garden-door, just as I was preparing to say good-night to her, my sister said that she was coming upstairs with me, that she would not get a wink of sleep unless she could hear the end of the story, that, at all costs, she must see Augustin again. I tried to dissuade her, warning her that he might say something offensive, that, in any case, he was probably in bed. Even if he weren't would he consent to gratify her whim? But all she would say was that she was prepared to run the risk. The staircase windows were noisy under the impact of the driving rain. Our candle-flames flickered on the pitch-pine panelling. No light showed under my door. 'He must be asleep' —I whispered. Then, as I hesitated before opening the door, Florence, with an impatient gesture, turned the handle. The bed had not been opened, and I saw at a glance that there was no sign of Augustin's clothes or books. I looked at Florence. I saw the disappointment in her face, and, in her hand, the lightless lamp of one of the foolish virgins.

VII

WE did not see him again. What more I have to say of him I got from the Superior (I was always a good hand at worming secrets out of him). But if we *did* make a fool of Augustin, then all I can say is that he took a subtle vengeance—and one bearing the undoubted marks of his authorship! Admittedly, Florence had reached, through him, the paradise of her dreams—marriage with one of the Sons, with the smartest of them all: but not until Augustin the sorcerer had used his philtres to disenchant her. On the very threshold of her false happiness, her eyes had been opened: she knew now, and had tasted the bitterness of disillusionment. . . . Poor wife to be! From the way in which you looked at that paunchy fool already going bald, at the inner emptiness revealed by a face of which the monocle was the only distinguishing mark, I could see that no coloured prism of illusion or of vanity would help you to endure having anything to do with him. As to matters of social precedence . . . how could I possibly think that there was still anything in them to charm you, now that I knew how, on the very day of the official betrothal, you had run about the town under a relentless downpour, questioning cab-drivers and sailors? But no one could tell you where the tall young man had gone.

Since then you have listened in silence to Maucoudinat's stable-talk; you have expressed admiration of his ability to pick, unerringly, an 1893 Margaux from ten different wines; you have seen to it that your furniture comes from Maple's, and that there shall be upon your walls engravings of race-horses (all looking like spiders). The lacquered Louis XV room has met with your approval; you have spared a smile for *l'Escarpolette* and *le Verrou* which strike—the phrase was your fiancé's—an elegantly naughty note. The Lubin Travel Agency supplied the itinerary of your wedding-trip.

I remember one particular October afternoon which was so dark and gloomy that the lamps had to be lit at three o'clock. Florence had received me in her boudoir, in spite of the fact that it was her 'at home' day. My aunt was only too delighted to take that tiresome duty over from her. Cackle worthy of a poultry-run came from the drawing-room. Paler, and, as it seemed to me, smaller than she had been, Florence was smiling at a letter lying open on her lap. She held it out to me, and I saw at once from the squared paper and the illiterate hand, that it was anonymous. Some kindly soul thought it not right that my sister should remain in ignorance of the fact that Monsieur Harry Maucoudinat was still carrying on a liaison with a former mistress whom he still adored.

'It is the first piece of real happiness he has given me,' said Florence.

She added (with that laugh of hers which was now, as ever, sneering and ill-natured):

'If you happen to know the woman in question, I should feel obliged if you would tell her how grateful I am. You will scarcely believe it, but let me tell you that in the days when he was still the adoring young husband, he actually asked me to forgive him! . . . It was worse than in the most bee-utiful moments of our honeymoon. But, thank God, he hasn't been home, the last two nights, until the early hours, and then in a state of complete exhaustion.'

I did not know what answer to make. Each time that the drawing-room across the hall opened, the silence was shattered by the clucking of hens, which, when it was shut again, dropped to a continuous murmur (because the ladies were all talking at the same time, making simultaneous and identical complaints about their servants). Without looking up, Florence asked whether I had been back to my old school. I told her that I had been too completely wrapped up in the delights of my first year as a law-student, for the idea of such a pilgrimage to appeal to me. She said that I was ill requiting the many kindnesses shown me by the Superior. She spoke with calculated indifference, but that did not keep me from realizing what lay behind her introduction of the subject. She had crumpled the anonymous letter in her right hand. I flattered myself that I could see the way her mind was working, and knew whither the conversation was tending. Far from helping her, I played the dunce, and she soon gave up beating about the bush. Without actually mentioning Augustin's name, she said, in a few hurried words, that only the Superior could tell me the end of the story to which we had listened one wild day of the preceding summer, at an inn beside the sea.

'It won't be the same thing, of course, as hearing it from him ... all the same ...'

Since she left the sentence unfinished, I thought it as well to express her thoughts aloud:

'At least, we shall learn whether he is alive or dead.'

That, she said, did not much matter, and I saw her smile sadly at my astonishment. To be sure, I did believe that she had conceived a belated passion for the fugitive, but, if that were so, why should she be so little interested to know whether he was still living? Nevertheless, this indifference on her part would not, alone, have been sufficient to make me realize my mistake. Even were she in love—having lost Augustin for ever, and since life would more surely separate them than the grave—Florence would have preferred the feeling of security which the death of the beloved gives to lovers without hope, the treasured assurance that he no longer lives and moves and has his being among others. For lovers like to think that *he* does not, as time passes, overlay old memories with new faces and fresh impressions, that, in short the adored image has remained alive and powerful to the end. . . . Once Florence had fallen a prey to passion, the childlike and untamed ferocity of her nature would, I felt, be quite capable of entertaining such feelings. But, on the day in question, while she tried with fumbling words, to open her heart to me, I realized that she did not see Augustin in the light either of a husband or a lover (to my single allusion to such a possibility she had replied with a burst of laughter in which I thought I could detect an underlying feeling of disgust)—but as the object of her fervent veneration, as the miracle-worker who had freed her from her bonds, and opened her eyes to the truth that the things of this world were utterly without interest for her. Because of him she knew now that her heart had escaped from captivity and become a fierce, wild thing. What did it matter that her body was chained in the prison of marriage? She told me that she was waiting only for a sign from destiny, to take to her heels, and I saw then that it is a good thing for women to grow embittered over questions of social precedence, that it is good for them to be bound by conventions, no matter how absurd.

We ended that day with the shadow of Augustin between us. I thought it essential that I should recall every one of my memories, beginning with that morning when he had come into the fifth-form room, and shaken hands with the Superior (who, no doubt, had snatched him like an eaglet from its

nest after his father had sought refuge in a Trappist monastery).
I was conscious that nothing about that strange young creature
had escaped my notice, that, unknown to myself, I had watched
him live and suffer. I could satisfy Florence's craving with a
recital of even the tiniest details, not one of which was without
importance. I tracked them down with infinite patience, and
even now, for my solitary delight, can fix them at the sound of
a chant, at the whiff of a fragrance. On that day, with Florence
there before me, they started with the beginning of a pale
October term when schoolboys feel at the furthest possible
remove from sun-drenched beaches, from the park where the
heat is so intense that one cannot venture into it until after
four-o'clock tea. In that season the full rigours of winter seem
already present, though it has scarcely yet begun . . . and ahead
there stretches the grey density of the school year blazed with the
glittering splendours of the great feasts of the Church. I remember Augustin on just such a day, under the shelter in the
playground. The pouring rain, and a sense of emptiness,
seemed to hedge him in. Oafish boys fondly imagined that
they were sending him to Coventry, though, in fact, it was he
who had imposed on them his private isolation. That he was
lonely depended on no activity of others. He was like a moun-
tain peak, which looks close enough to be reached in a morning's walk, though, after hours of tedious climbing, it is still
where it was, one with the radiance of the setting sun, covered
in its flushed mantle of snow, near at hand, but virginal and
inaccessible.

I reminded Florence of that impassive face which, one evening, I had seen, for the first time, bathed in tears—and all
because of her. Humiliated, conscious how unworthy she had
been, Florence hung her head. Doubtless, thought I, under the
influence of my reading at the time—it was only by loading

her with his own riches, that Augustin had been able to love that little slave. . . . He had made her the trustee of all he had within himself of feminine weakness. It is always ourselves we love. . . .

Florence sent word that she would not go down to dinner. The maid brought a cold supper to her room, and we ate it in the glow of candles. At midnight I was still talking about Augustin. I talked on, to a young woman who was hanging on my words.

VIII

NEXT day I was walking along the road which led to the school. It was two o'clock in the afternoon (I had pretended to be far from well all morning, giving as my excuse a difficult mathematical problem, but now, having been betrayed by a hearty appetite at luncheon, I had found it necessary, as soon as the last mouthful was swallowed, to turn my steps in this direction). Once past the boulevards, I sauntered down a suburban street from which I could already see, like rising smoke against the autumn sky, the bare branches of the trees which stood about my old school. Though but a few weeks separated me from the years which I had spent there, between it and me were now, and ever would be, the nights when I had played my part in the squalid orgies of the Sons. But champagne, a mechanical piano, and big Marcelle had proved, alas, to be no sure defence against the clarity of mind which Augustin had left with me when he departed. Since those days, I have learned that in Paris there exists a sort of poetry of bars, each having its own particular smell, its own especial clientèle, that the poor successors of 'les poètes maudits' have their own haunts where they mingle their fumy genius with the smell of tobacco and the stench of spirits. There was nothing of that kind in the city where the Sons of the Great Houses thought it a fine thing to pay a louis a bottle for champagne which could add nothing to their general condition of sottishness. I did nothing, however, to eschew their company, finding that so much baseness helped me to live. Without them

I should have found myself alone upon the shore where Augustin had abandoned me, faced by a temptress sea I could not cross, the foamy tracks of which, he used to say, led to the Infinite Being—alone and unsupported at the heart of a great wind of Pentecost. How necessary are the rules of precedence! Their trivial hierarchies hedge us in; the blinkers keep us all from feeling giddy; the water-tight compartments offer us the blessed refuge of immobility; the little labels stuck on our backs save us from having to find a formula elsewhere. The absolute is suited only to a few human spirits. I watched Florence slowly burning herself up because the cork rafts of imbecile convention no longer served to keep her afloat. I had no wish to die; I was afraid of God, and hid from him in a darkness of debauchery which was made more dense by the company of inferior and degraded beings. Pascal, I told myself, had seen pleasure as something that should, quite literally, be a 'distraction', something that could keep men from thinking of their destiny. But that is no less true of social shibboleths. Their tortured, Chinese complexities distract us from the one thing necessary. Our vanity constructs these trivial dykes. We build them as children build castles of sand, squatting on the beach with their backs to the sea.

From these reflections (which, it must be admitted, were remarkable in a young man of my age) I roused myself at the very entrance to the school. The spoon-shaped face of the porter welcomed me with the smile he kept for 'old boys'. In summer a buzz of bees would have sounded through the twenty open windows, but now the misty October day seemed to wrap the great lit building in layers of cotton-wool. I crossed the black-and-white paved entrance-hall (in the old days I had always been careful to tread only on the white squares, because the least false step would have meant that I was not in a state of grace). From the honeycomb of classrooms as I passed came the carefully articulated and repeated words of a dictation, or a timid jumble of Greek, or that most excruciating of all the many sounds, the breaking of a stick of chalk, and a finger-nail scraping the blackboard. I stopped outside the door of the fifth cell, within which a child's voice was reciting that tale of Florian, *l'Enfant et la Sarigue*. A very young and grubby boarder had been sent out into the passage, and, with his mouth against the window-pane was amusing himself by making circles of vapour. I asked his name, and he said, 'Jean Queyries.'

The third floor was filled with a smell of chemicals, but on the fourth, where the chapel is, a scent of aromatics greeted me. It was so strong that I halted. I sniffed and I listened. As always, some young priest was in there, seeking consolation for his lonely heart by playing on the wheezy old harmonium in the dark. Next to the Sacristy is the Head-master's study. Instinctively I knocked with a crooked forefinger, as I had done, only a year before, when going to confession. The Superior uttered a cry of pleasure, took both my hands in his, and looked me up and down. Of the two of us it was he who had the clear eyes of the adolescent. I turned away my own less innocent ones.

The good old man wasted much time on trivialities, but I could not long keep from letting my friend's name fall between us. He expressed astonishment at my being without news: he, himself, had had some recent information from a missionary who had been to see him on his way back from Senegal. I learned that Augustin was out there, engaged in bartering bead necklaces and coloured cotton stuffs for ground-nuts. He had, from the very first, taken to this trading with a quite extraordinary enthusiasm. The climate, which drives most white men crazy, or kills them, seemed, on the contrary, to have tempered him, body and soul. Then, later, a great peace had descended upon him, or, rather, said the Superior (showing a subtler insight than I should have given him credit for) the peace which had always existed deep down in him, had come to the surface. Augustin had made contact with some Missionary Fathers. Africa, he said, with its consumed and arid landscape, did far less than our damper climate to separate men from the Infinite Being. He gloried in the fact that, having been condemned from his cradle to be not of this world, there had been no need for him to renounce it; with feet firmly on the ground, and face to face with the object of his search, he had gone straight forward, only occasionally seeing it hidden from him when, in certain brief intervals, the flesh had been too weak. He might well think himself forearmed now against the assaults of passion. While he had still been scarcely more than a schoolboy, an all-powerful will had taken apart, before his eyes, like some complicated and troublesome piece of machinery, the female heart and all its wiles.

'Augustin,' went on the Superior, 'has had good reason to bless Him who saw to it that he should be born outside all castes, hierarchies and social shibboleths. This being an outlaw from the world of men had brought salvation to his father, as well. I knew him in the days when he occupied an important chair at the Catholic University of N . . . , when, though a simple layman, he was already acclaimed as a Master, and had Princes of the Church sitting at his feet, making notes of what he said. More than any ecclesiastic he concerned himself with matters of teaching and administration. Whole seminaries, though the Bishop did not know it, were in the habit of receiving, and acting upon, his directives. Often,

when I went to see him, I would find the valiant Senator of
Z . . . , the famous leader, X . . . sitting patiently on kitchen
chairs in his anteroom, with stuffed brief-cases on their laps,
and their feet on the crossbars to keep them clear of the chill
which rose from the tiled floor. All the same, that revered
teacher had been no more capable of resisting the lures of the
flesh than he had been of disciplining the pride of the intellect.
He had yielded to the threefold seduction of the abbé Loisy,
Father Tyrrell, and a young Polish woman. His wife, a most
charming woman (and the daughter of a Member of the
Institute) had been unable to control him, as had, too, his
children. Rejected, placed under the Papal ban, spewed out by
his familiars, outlawed by his social equals, a suspect even in
the eyes of his chosen colleagues, he had cast aside every
worldly formula, every convention, and had found himself
stripped of everything that might serve to bind him to his
fellow men. No one raised their hats to him in the street, no
letters came to him. An exile from all the hierarchies, he had
become a homeless wanderer. And then, abandoned by the
world, the Truth had once more seized him by the throat. . . .'
(Listening to the Superior, I could see, in imagination, the
man whom Augustin had described to us, seated at his table,
surrounded by books as by a pitiless pack of hounds.) . . .
'After years of agony'—went on the Superior—'he was little
more than a game-bird harried by Grace. Loss of social status
saved the renegade. Now, crucified and reduced to the most
abject poverty, he is suffering with a joyful heart in the
Trappist House of S. . . . When his legitimate wife died, he
might have aspired to priestly vows. Perhaps he thought that
he was still unworthy. Be that as it may, he is still no more than
a lay-brother attached to the monastery. I am told that his
main task is looking after those who go there to make a retreat,

and that he is resigned to never seeing his son again. To sum up, the two of them, father and son, have served to point the way to you, dear lad.'

I protested that God does not insist on all men renouncing the world. . . .

'But, my child, no one is forbidden to love the world.'

In such words did the Superior speak to me. A striking clock broke in upon him, and I had to take my leave.

I stopped at one of the windows in the corridor. I could hear the babble of boys coming out of school, but my thoughts were all on what I had been told and now treasured in my heart. I relapsed into a fit of brooding. From all greatness of spirit I was kept by squalid excesses and the rites of my caste. Inferior persons hedged me in, keeping me at their own level. They dictated the gestures I should make, the mistress I should have, the tailor I should frequent. With each day that passed, I was reducing my spiritual stature, silencing my inner voice. In matters of horses, women, the common herd ('of no possible interest') and religion ('useful for keeping the servants from thieving') I had to abide by their formulae. If *they* rejected me what should I have left? The idiot regiment of these men encompassed me, protecting me from that Hunter with whose relentless activities Augustin's father was only too familiar, whom my friend, freed from the world, had chosen as alone worthy of his love. That love I did not want. Not with that tragic issue would I burden my own destiny. In vain did the angel seek me out. I refused to wrestle with him. . . .

The four strokes of the clock filled the classrooms with the din of slamming desks. Outside, one of the school servants was setting baskets of bread at the gates of the different yards. Hurriedly I fled from these reminders of the past which was still too close to me in time not to exercise a charm. The suburban road was filled with the light and the smells which I associated with the joy of those afternoons when, on rare occasions, we had been let out at four. I walked slowly past the railings of the leafless gardens. I was reminded of a walk that I had taken with Augustin when, with a mechanical gesture, he had let his fingers run along the uprights as though they had been the strings of a harp. The strange background of his life, I told myself, had kept him free from all rigid patterns and classifications. But only to a few is it given to tread the heights, to join the company of the great Solitaries. I had no such pretentions, nor did I wish to have, and Florence, I thought, had no reason either to aspire to such a state. That was why I planned, without further delay, to stimulate in her a taste for subtle social differentiations.

I felt sure that I should find her seated beside the fire. At first, when I told her that I had just come back from the school, I saw that she was concentrating her mind to take in what I might have to tell her, but, at the first words I uttered, a look of disappointment in her face showed clearly that she no longer expected anything from me. I stopped in the middle of what I was saying, and reminded her that there had been a time when she attached great importance to her position in society, pointing out that she must not go on despising what so unparalleled a situation offered unless she wanted to bring ridicule upon the members of our group. After all, there was no reason why we should not open our charmed circle to a few people of intelligence, in short, establish a salon.

For a long time I discoursed eloquently on this theme, but her silence defeated my fluency. In the darkness the half-burned logs among the ashes showed with a livelier glow. I could see nothing but the outline of her bowed figure. What madness to cheat myself into believing that I could any longer pull the wool over eyes which, from now on, could not but be clear-sighted! Only some mystical experience could offer a haven for that drifting and dismasted heart. But Florence, no matter how completely detached she might have become from matters of protocol and precedence, was still a carnal creature. The taste of Perfection meant nothing to her: she was utterly indifferent to the things of the spirit. Why, oh why, was she not a sister of that Jacqueline Pascal who would never allow that there could be any limit to chastity? Had she been, then, perhaps, she might have led me, her weak young brother, to God. . . . Alas! there are more ways than one of renouncing the world, of openly breaking free of its conventions. I had a strong presentiment, after that evening, that Florence would find her way of escape in mad and foolish love affairs. To these she did, indeed, quite soon abandon herself, but I do not suppose that anyone expects me to be their chronicler.

PART TWO

*' . . . Nothing can console us for the
loss of what once seemed infinite . . . '*

BALZAC

I

Monday evening: 21st February, 19 . . . .

AFTER twelve years I have found hidden away in a drawer the notebook which I had pretended to forget. 'That is the end of the story'—I had told myself, as though a story is ever ended! All that happens is that ashes cover up the heart, but under them, all through the passing years, the fire still smoulders. The drama takes a new turn, but the adolescents of its earlier scenes now show as old, and physically deteriorated. In the springtime of life Sin does not show in a man's face. That season is secure from soiling. But, to-day, when we talk together, our eyes try not to meet. Would it not be better, then, to keep silent? But the fact that so many pages in that book are still blank shows me that destiny is still at work.

Jean Queyries, to whom I had sent a message that I wanted very urgently to see him, has telephoned to say that he will look in after the Gala Performance at the Grand Theatre. My window stands open to the deserted quays where cranes stretch motionless black arms towards the sky, though the cries of the early swifts have not yet heralded the torpor of the stifling nights. Before Jean makes his appearance, looking younger than ever, slimmer than ever, in his evening clothes, but a little too correct, stiff, starched, and, at first sight, incapable of any mad and impulsive behaviour, it is well that I should turn my eyes inwards and try to disentangle the many reasons why I want to see him. At school I had already, under

77

instruction from my director, learned how, pen in hand, to set down an examination of my conscience. I am now about to use the same method, not to open a way to sanctity, but the better to understand my motives.

My familiarity with Jean Queyries, who is employed as junior traveller for 'our' wine business, needs some explaining. One can be both traveller and man of the world. Here, wine confers nobility, and if a traveller cannot be said to have attained to the same high rank as a wholesaler, as the head of one of the Great Houses, he still takes precedence of the liberal professions, and of the rank and file of civil servants. But Jean Queyries is the son of a cooper, and the obscurity of his origins should keep me from having any social contacts with him. God knows there are plenty of reasons why I should watch my step, why, more than any other young man of my world, I should keep my distance. No more than Jean Queyries, was I born to the purple. It was not that sacred product, wine, that enriched my ancestors, but cloth, but timber, everything that is most looked down upon. I am of your kin, Monsieur Jourdain, of yours, Monsieur Dimanche, of yours, Monsieur Poirier. It goes without saying that the splendid marriage, now some ten years old, which my sister, Florence, made with young Harry Maucoudinat—of Maucoudinat and Tanenbaum—opened to us the doors of James Castaingt, of the Willy Durands, the John Martineaus, the Fredy Duponts, the Bertie Dupont-Gunthers and the Percy Larousselles. I was even made the recipient of a favour unique—I think—in our town: I was elected to the *London and Westminster Club*, though the name of none of my forebears shines resplendent in the Golden Book of high commerce. I am under an obligation not to lose caste. True, our good fortune has been bought at the cost of many enmities. We had to resign ourselves to sacrificing cousins who were really not presentable, old connections who would have brought disgrace upon us in 'that world'. Our conduct in this matter gave birth to many patient hatreds which grow only stronger with the passage of time. To judge by appearances there is no sign, you will say, of the remotest threat to our glory. That is to some extent true. At the recent funeral of my uncle, the presence of all the Heads, of all the Sons, of the great families gave us the measure of our social prominence. Remembering the many gaps in the ranks of those who gathered about my aunt's coffin only two years ago, we had every reason, standing with our feet in frozen mud, but with burning pride in our hearts, to wonder at the distance we had come. Such unanimity almost spoiled our happiness. 'The thing is beginning to look like a demonstration'—I said to myself: 'they wouldn't have put on a show like this for one of themselves!'—for the hearse had trailed behind it, like a black and shining caterpillar, the two hundred and twenty silk hats of the *London and Westminster*. 'What a pity,' said my sarcastic sister, Florence, 'that the old gentleman isn't here to see it all and count them!' She laughed rather loudly, and I begged her to stop.

We owe our acceptance by 'that world' to Florence, but how uncomfortable her freakish outbursts make us! I had sworn to myself, Florence, to pretend ignorance of your excesses: after all, why should I show more interest in such matters than my Maucoudinat brother-in-law?—especially since, at first, there was nothing in them to worry us. I don't think I need labour the point—all I mean is that her 'fancies' did not send her straying beyond the frontiers of our world. Indeed, I would go so far as to say that her latest adventure has added to the lustre which her marriage brought us, for there are irregular unions so flattering that the family of the woman in the case finds in them more than one advantage usually reserved for more permanent arrangements. I don't want to be misunderstood. There was certainly no scheming on Florence's part about its inception. The days have long gone by when the idea of social privilege could carry any weight with her. No: to speak quite frankly, the chance directions taken by her amorous proclivities have, until last autumn, been of very considerable service to us. It is difficult to overrate the prestige we have enjoyed as a result of her intimacy with Percy Larousselle.

That scion of one of the most important of the great families —he has the unusual distinction of combining the traffic in rum with the wine business—is, in his own person, a unique specimen—in fact, in the club he is known as the 'Phenomenon.' To cut a long story short, he professes to be knowledgeable about the latest publications. Speaking for myself, I have so far had to hide my taste in matters literary as though it were a vice. But that is far from being the case where Percy Larousselle is concerned. Admittedly, the indulgent attitude of his peers is largely due to his readiness to submit to the rites and conventions of our world. Books in no way interfere with his interest in cards, horses and women. All things considered, his library plays a smaller part in his life than does his stable and his little love-nest. It would be manifestly unfair to tax him with erudition, or even with culture. His taste in books runs to the hermetic. I like to let my memory dwell on certain evenings I have spent with Percy on the verandah of our villa at Gravette. There we would sit, dividing our attention between a play by Claudel and a decanter of brandy so rare and precious that the stopper was secured by a miniature silver padlock, the key to which my friend always carried on his person.

I read and he drank, and in the pauses of these twin activities, we listened to the waves breaking gently against the garden wall. Clouds in the evening sky made endless patterns which, for a brief moment, seemed to body forth the poet's fancies.

Florence, emerging from one of those periods of dejection and disgust to which she is prone, would sit listening to my reading, and, so lively a pleasure did she find in it, that she renewed the experience, first with me, then without me, and finally, though I did not know it at the time, behind my back. She combined literature, alcohol and love-making much as the sophisticated find enchantment in the discovery of a new cocktail.

Had Percy Larousselle ever fathomed the cause of the favours with which she honoured him, his pride might well have suffered. Because as a young girl, she had got to know a boy in whom there was a continuous murmur of all the poems of all the poets, those which Percy read to her seemed, in her ears, to retain the very inflexions of that marvellous voice to which she had listened in the old days. But, after the passage of so many years, I alone remembered that Augustin about whom my sister no longer even spoke to me, though I did not for a moment doubt that she was still dreaming of the vanished wanderer. While I sit writing all this, I can hear the sound of sirens in the harbour, and so it is that through the density of the past your voice, Augustin, comes back to me—the voice of a poor boy who, at school, was addressed only by his Christian name, though his companions, all of them the products of rich families, enjoyed the splendour of names which recall the labels on the bottles of noble vintages—a pariah whom the secret of your birth isolated less than your ability to understand everything, and that taste you had for silence and for loneliness, that prejudice of yours in favour of always being punished, of remaining aloof from the company of the Sons. . . .

Percy Larousselle's library attracted Florence, because there she could read the names which a youth named Augustin had taught her to love almost twelve years before. How should I not have known of the survival in my sister's memory of a youth now vanished, I, who, deep in my heart, could still evoke his image and still keep alive my mourning for a dead friendship? If I allow Jean Queyries to visit me so often of an evening, a man who belongs neither to my world nor to my generation, and who bores me, let me here confess the ridiculous reason that enables me to put up with him: it is that he has a strange resemblance to Augustin—in face I mean. But, more than that, his voice has the same inflexions. God knows that in other ways, this shrewd and matter-of-fact young man has nothing in him that is in the least like that mad, adventurous creature who was my schoolmate. Jean Queyries could never understand the mysterious sympathy which he awakes in me, even if I were willing to explain it. He is convinced that I have a feeling of friendship for him. He has none for me, nor, indeed for anybody. But in his eyes I am an extremely valuable acquaintance. Though incapable of friendship—which is a disinterested emotion—he is more than capable of love, or, perhaps I should say, of desire. Jean Queyries dreams of Florence as Ruy Blas dreamed of the Queen of Spain. Those who are familiar with the social conventions of this town will have no difficulty in realizing that a petty commercial-traveller is as far removed from Madame Maucoudinat as an earth-worm is from a star. Over and above all this, he is madly ambitious, and longs to be given the entrée to our world. If the practical-minded Jean Queyries still keeps the flame of our friendship alive, the reason is that he lives in hope of one day paying court to Florence, and, through her, of reaching the gateway of that paradise where sit enthroned the Heads of the great

Families and their Sons. Fair indeed is the life, which begins with love and ambition. He sees that I like talking with him, and thinks that I might be weak enough to help him. Realizing that by introducing him into the Maucoudinat circle I should be playing high and risking my own position, he fully understands why it is that I go on beating about the bush. Still, he is patient and has made up his mind to wait. Only the other day I was laughing at his bumptiousness. How could he ever dream of my introducing a boy born of the People into the company of the Sons? You have been counting on a miracle, Jean Queyries, and, alas! you are right. This evening, I shall speak the words you have so long been hoping to hear. The moment is approaching when I shall take you by the hand and lead you to the object of your young passion. A series of circumstances has inevitably forced me to wish for the very thing that, yesterday, would have seemed fraught with peril. I will set them down on paper, doubtless for my own pleasure, doubtless, too, as a result of my curiosity about myself and others, but also in the hope that, by doing so, I may be able to see my way clearly at this turning-point of my life where a single false step would set me plunging into that outer darkness peopled by crawling things which have nothing to do with my world.

II

PERCY buys first editions when he has reason to believe that they will go on increasing in value. One can be interested in a book published in an edition of five copies on hand-made paper, without necessarily having to read it. He has a blind adoration of all limited issues, and studies booksellers' catalogues with the same care that he gives to Stock-Exchange prices. He excels in the blending of different varieties of alcohol, and knows exactly how to lighten the sugary thickness of Kummel by adding to it a certain quantity of old brandy. In much the same way he can achieve that state of blissful enjoyment so necessary for the understanding of unintelligible geniuses. Florence, in spite of her habitual dreaminess, is terribly clear-sighted. Neither Percy nor his library can any longer take her in, though that does not mean that their liaison would have come to an early end since it is unlikely that the pleasure it brought her was of a purely literary kind. No, what really finished it was the influence of the deplorable woman who was installed in the Maucoudinat home to act as governess to my niece, Eliane.

I well remember the February day when we saw her for the first time. We were just finishing luncheon. Maucoudinat had sent for those wide-brimmed glasses which the Sons use for wine-tasting. He filled his own and Percy's. They both stuck their noses into them at one and the same moment, then, after sniffing in concert, raised the precious liquid to catch the sun and set its ruby colour sparkling, agreeing on the perfect condition of that particular 1893 Léoville, while, in the small pantry constructed for the purpose, they rinsed their glasses in readiness for another test. An acute sense of tact saved me from imitating these rites. If the Sons have been so very kind as to feign ignorance of my origins, it is not for me to prod their memory. Florence, as usual, was remote, silent, and miles removed from this tasting ceremony. The footman came in to tell her that a lady had arrived with whom she had arranged an interview. Florence informed us, with a look of complete exhaustion, that Madame Fredy Dupont had recommended this person as a suitable governess for Eliane, but that she felt in no fit state to make decisions. She asked us to let her have the woman shown into the dining-room so that we might help her in making up her mind.

Then and there appeared, with crape veil thrown back, a drawn and ravaged face framed in grey locks of hair. The newcomer, four of whose fingers showed through holes in her thread gloves, was clutching an umbrella one of the bent ribs of which caught in the curtain which hangs before the door. Harry Maucoudinat turned on Florence the terrible glare of his after-luncheon face. Percy, with both elbows on the table, in that unceremonious attitude which here goes by the name of British, went on picking his teeth. He managed to save the operation from appearing vulgar by keeping his monocle in place while it was proceeding. He failed to stifle a laugh, and the sound made me feel that I should die of shame. But the governess did not hear it. She began to speak in rapturous tones which had to be heard to be believed.

'I saw Eliane in the hall, madame, and I can assure you that she has already won my heart. Nothing is more false than the proverb which warns us not to judge people at first sight. Your daughter's seraphic eyes have completely conquered me. It is clear that she is terrifyingly intelligent.'

This time, Percy burst into a guffaw. Eliane was one of those children of whom their parents say, making the best of a bad job, that something wrong with their eyes prevents them from learning to read, that a quite extraordinary shyness paralyses them as soon as a stranger tries to teach them anything, though the fact of the matter is that she is a little fool, which is what people mean when they say—'she could, but she won't make the effort.' The visitor kept nodding her head with a beatific smile. To change the subject, I remarked in a funeral voice, that her deep mourning no doubt betokened a recent loss. At that her rapture faded.

'I have been shedding tears for the loss of M. Etinger for close on eighteen years. He had the most wonderful eyes in the world, unique eyes. Would you believe it; one day on the beach at Biarritz, a lady took my daughter in her arms, and said: "There cannot be three pairs of such eyes: you must be the child of Oscar Etinger!" The world treated my husband harshly, sir. It was not for me to forgive him, since I had not been called to sit in judgment. That is how I am made. An old friend, who was, in some sort, a lay director to me, used frequently to say: "Madame Etinger is a woman who takes a lofty view." I was grateful to M. Etinger even for the manner of his death. His end was that of a gentleman, for he had made up his mind to die in evening-dress with a gardenia in his button-hole, such as he wore every day, and the drama was played out in a bedroom at the Savoy. . . .'

The good lady was clearly somewhat wandering in her mind. My brother-in-law and Percy were chuckling away and digging each other in the ribs. But Florence and I were far from any thought of laughter. Deep within us there sounded the distant echo of that name—Etinger. The moment the governess had uttered it I had seen Florence grow pale.

'Is your name Madame Etinger?' she said in a low voice.

No doubt she, at that moment, was seeing, as I could see, across the vanished years, a melancholy beach under a lowering sky, where we had made Augustin reveal to us the secret of his life. Not a word spoken by that strange youth but was deeply etched into our minds. It is the privilege of certain human beings that everything they say continues, indefinitely, to echo in the hearts of those who heard them. He had told us that his father, after renouncing his beliefs and denying his faith, had but one faithful soul left to him—Madame Etinger. In telling us this, he had painted so cruel a portrait of the lady that, though we had never set eyes on her, we had, both of us, after such a long lapse of time, recognized her immediately. She had risen before us with every detail just as our friend had fixed her ineffaceably in our memories. It never occurred to us to doubt that this aged creature had been the actual witness of a life of which his fellow-men had known nothing, though its least circumstance meant as much to Florence and to me as would have done each gesture or each word of a hero or a god.

My sister had risen to her feet, had taken the lady's hand and given her a long and silent look. At last she said:

'You can have your luggage brought here, madame; your room shall be got ready.'

Madame Etinger picked up from the floor a small and very shabby black bag.

'This,' she said, 'is all the luggage I have. My one and only jewel I have left in a room at the Terminus Hotel.'

I told her it would be most unwise to let it stay there.

The look she gave me was not without a certain haughti-
ness:

'I was speaking of my daughter, sir. Spare me, I beg, your
unworthy insinuations.'

Draped in her faded crape, she gave a capital performance of
a woman wounded in her most sensitive spot, and made her
exit. Harry Maucoudinat nervously enquired of Florence
whether she really meant to entrust Eliane to this lunatic. In
the look she gave him there was so much contempt that my
brother-in-law, for all he was a Maucoudinat, could not help
exhibiting uneasiness. She did not answer him in words. While
I waited in the hall for Madame Etinger to be safely on the
other side of the street from where she could not direct her
lyrical outpourings on me, Florence said:

'As though it mattered two hoots about Eliane!'

It was the first time, for ten years, that she had made even
an indirect allusion to Augustin. She went on:

'I didn't dare ask her whether he is still alive, but I will,
as soon as she gets back. Let us wait for her.'

She sat down on a chest. In the semi-darkness her face and
hands looked ghastly. She made me sit beside her. We could
hear the servant putting away the silver, and, in the room above,
the sound of a sewing-machine. I remembered how, as a child,
I had sat for hours at a time on the wood-box. People crossing
the hall could not see me. Wholly isolated, I dreamed a thous-
and dramas with myself as hero. It was an extraordinary
sensation now, as a man of thirty, and in spite of the wear and
tear of time, of habits and of vices, to find myself withdrawn
into just such a patch of darkness, with the same old contraction
in my throat, the same sweating hands. How long was it since
I had felt any comparable surge of sentiment, any such sense
of contact with my sister? I put my arm round her neck and

kissed her cheek. It was wet, and had a salty taste. She was crying. I knew I must not utter a word, nor risk a gesture, but sit silently with her hand in mine. The sound of a cab on the cobbles reached our ears. Florence looked at me. We both knew instinctively that it would stop before our door. It did, and someone rang the bell. We went back to the drawing-room where the bright light hurt our eyes. Florence powdered her face and reddened her lips. But Madame Etinger did not come in at once: we could hear her ask the servant to show her to her room.

Though, for the last two hours, I had been on the look-out for her, I was, by now, so little consistent that I no longer even wished to see her. Florence's feverish restlessness was intolerable: it may be, too, that I dreaded having to know for certain. I remembered that, after the examination for the baccalauréat, I had waited all one afternoon at the Faculty for the list to be posted, and then made off a few seconds before it came. In just such a way did I hurry from the Maucoudinats' house. It looked on to the Public Gardens. I crossed the terrace where a marble statue stands which, at sixteen, I had found enchanting —a youth fondling a chimaera. It was one of those February evenings which, in this part of the world, already have about them the smell of spring. Nurses were gathering their charges together. The woman who sold rolls, her colleague who dealt in sugared oranges, and the goats, had all of them finished the day's work. On the sanded paths were the scrawled squares and numbers of children's games which the coming night would not efface. The chairs arranged in rows bore witness to a game of school. The temporary buildings put up for the Horse-Show still encumbered the Quinconces, and I could hear the sounds of applause, the blare of horns. The top-hat of some red-coated competitor showed above the barrier, and I could catch the smell of dung and straw and the ammoniac odour of horses. I walked on and reached the quays, where I live in a flat with a balcony. It may be the very one from which Baudelaire watched the rosy mists of evening rise before embarking on the *Paquebot-des-mers-du-Sud*. Night fell while I was still leaning on its rail. What kept me there was not the golden light upon the river, out towards the sea, nor yet the hubbub of the workers' trams when the air is heavy with a sense of lassitude and infinite weariness. What I could see then with my inner eye was Augustin as he had looked when I had seen him last, upright against a background of tempestuous sea, with the wind in his hair, and his face turned towards the stinging spray.

The ringing of the telephone roused me. I recognized Florence's voice: 'He may be still alive. He wrote to Madame Etinger early on in the war—he was in the Foreign Legion. . . . But after the Marne he gave no further sign.' She begged me not to see her again that evening, because we should not be able to keep from speaking of him, and this she did not want. As I replaced the receiver, my man-servant showed Jean Queyries into the room. Never before had I been so struck by his likeness to Augustin. Contrary to his usual habit, he had come to see me straight from work, without bothering to brush his hair or change his collar. His shirt was crumpled; there was an untidy lock of hair hanging over his forehead. . . . I felt myself grow pale at seeing there before me the very image of one we had known so well and hurt so deeply, of a vanished youth who might, to-day, still be in the land of the living.

Meanwhile, Jean Queyries had started to say something to me:

'Just as I was leaving the office, I ran into young James

Castaingt. You know, don't you, that I was introduced to him at the *Lion rouge*? I waved my hand, but he didn't seem to recognize me. He's a bit short-sighted, isn't he?'

I replied that intermittent short-sightedness was a birthright of the Sons.

III

THROUGHOUT the following days the subject of Augustin did not, in fact, arise between Florence and myself, though the presence of Madame Etinger meant that he was never for long out of our minds. It was suddenly as though Percy Larousselle had never existed so far as my sister was concerned. He found it convenient to go to London to take orders and to attend a tasting. Maucoudinat again began to find home boring, and reverted to what is a regular habit of the Sons—taking every other meal with their mistresses. It is only fair to point out that Madame Etinger, funereal and loquacious, would have frightened any man away. It had been suggested that she should take her meals apart with Eliane, but she had at once invoked the memory of her husband who would never, she said, have consented to her being treated as an underling. Eliane was left free to eat with her fingers, and elicited nothing from her governess but praise.

'It is not for me, dear child, to blame you for a natural tendency to dreaming, which the vulgar call going about with your head in the clouds. I am, myself, only too prone to indulging in that weakness, as was M. Etinger. I can best describe him to you, sir, by saying that it would never occur to him to make petty economies. I have known him, at Mentone, refuse to take the train which is a standing reproach to that beautiful coast. When he went to Nice it was always in a carriage drawn by four horses. My daughter has inherited his taste for expensive living, and she must do me the justice to admit that even when things with me were most difficult, I never failed to provide her with every delicacy. I well remember one Christmas day when, harassed by a pack of insolent and unreasonable trades-people, I presented her with a pineapple fit for an empress. In spite of the fact that such luxuries compelled me to move constantly from one district to another, and even from town to town—for greengrocers and poulterers are among the most insolent creatures it has ever been my misfortune to encounter—I felt that I owed it to my husband's memory to maintain a high standard.'

She turned to each of us in turn her grey and wrinkled face, fully expecting to hear from us a condemnation of such foolish extravagance. She pushed back the white locks from her forehead, and there was a look of challenge in her eyes. But we expressed approval of her conduct, and I was so weak as to deplore Eva's inability to dine with us that evening. This well-intentioned remark of mine merely had the effect of irritating her. 'You take pleasure, sir, in the spectacle of my misfortunes. It amuses you to know that Eva occupies the post of Secretary to Maître Balisac. She has sent word that she must spend this evening in copying a number of documents which are needed in connection with an important piece of litigation.'

Though Madame Etinger had told us more than once that she took the most exalted view of everything, it needed some effort of the imagination so to regard the position occupied by her daughter in the establishment of Maître Balisac who, for close on half a century has enjoyed the reputation of being the best, but most dissolute, lawyer in town. He has the secret of retaining a youthful figure, and, by a discreet use of dye, of avoiding the ravages of time. He is unique as a lawyer in having the entrée to the world of Big Business, though, admittedly, he is treated with the easy condescension shown to pettifogging attorneys by stage aristocrats. Eva may have been a bit of a loose fish, but, for all that, Florence and I sincerely regretted her absence, knowing, as we did, that as a small girl in a Paris suburb, she had played on a balcony with Augustin. Not that she ever spoke to us of those days. Florence, doubtless, had questioned both mother and daughter, though in such a way as to conceal from them the interest we felt in the young man, and, in any case the two women had had so adventurous a life that the episode of Augustin's father was unlikely to have left much of an impression upon them. I was particularly careful not to provoke remarks which would only have put a drag on the secret working of my imagination. Eva wore her hair short, and nobody, looking at her, would have guessed that she would never see thirty again. She had a thin, sallow face, with elongated, tired-looking eyes and a bitter, greedy mouth. We were for ever trying to probe into her past, for to us she was like a mirror in which we hoped to see reflected the beloved features of one now dead. That was why we felt a certain degree of affection for her, the woman who, as a little girl, on a suburban balcony, had once, to the accompaniment of twittering swifts and grinding trams, played with a small boy called Augustin.

A week passed during which I waited on tenterhooks for catastrophe. Each of my sister's liaisons had a way of calming her mad moods and temporarily steadying her, and those periods were the only ones when I could sleep without having nightmares. In between I can scarcely be said to have lived at all. The state of feverish excitement to which the companionship of Madame Etinger provoked my sister, appeared to me to be a fruitful soil for tragedy. On the Friday following that lady's arrival among us, the threat of danger was forced on my attention so suddenly that I could do nothing to ward it off. There was a Gala night at the Grand Theatre, and we, as a matter of course, were there. We had dined earlier than usual, and Harry Maucoudinat, as sometimes happened, had chosen that evening to make us sample several different wines. Florence showed no dislike of the performance. I noticed how brightly her eyes were shining, and that the rouge on her cheeks was quite unnecessary. We entered the theatre to be at once enveloped in the moonlit atmosphere of *Werther*. One of the pleasing aspects of life in our provincial capital is that one can take pleasure in that type of music without fear of arousing contempt. In Paris one has to pretend that one cannot endure it. With the best will in the world it is impossible to follow all the shifts and changes of 'good taste'. The interval is especially agreeable once one is assured that none of the boxes contains people who deliberately avoid one's eyes. Endless are the tricks and stratagems one witnesses, but to detail them would serve no purpose since they are identical with those noticed by Henri Beyle in La Scala at Milan, and in those other theatres up and down Italy where he ate ices and breathed in the fragrance of bare shoulders while the music set his passions freely working. Jean Queyries was no less susceptible than Stendhal. Wearing a short jacket and black tie, though sitting in the pit, he took advantage of his distance from us to keep his eyes fixed on Florence, though he was not so ill-bred as to show in public that he was acquainted with me.

On the evening in question I noticed, in the stalls, a man who kept making signs to me with his cane. These, at first, I set myself prudently to ignore. Despite our heroic efforts to weed them out, several of our former friends still stick like leeches, plague the life out of us, and obstinately refuse to take no for an answer, even when it is expressed in the rudest possible manner, the more so since Florence shows the utmost contempt for her grandeur, and treats unpresentable cousins with a kindliness which completely neutralizes the effect of my own bad manners.

In despair of attracting my attention, the unknown left his seat, and, a few seconds later, knocked at the door of our box. I nearly fainted with horror when I recognized him as a fellow called Hourtinat who had been famous for his strength at mathematics as also in the gymnasium. Though he was clean-shaven, there was a bluish tinge on his cheeks. His black hair, which looked almost blue, came so low down over his forehead that it nearly joined his eyebrows. This wild, hirsute vegetation flourished wherever it could find a lodgement. It swarmed over his wrists, gobbled up his finger-joints, sprouted from his ears and—incredible though it may seem—from his nose! His thick, baboon lips revealed, when parted, a full set of canines. Nevertheless, he was a fine figure of a man, with narrow eyes, wide shoulders and small hips, in short, the perfect lady-killer. While he was crushing my fingers in his great paw, I noticed, with a sort of stunned amazement that two enormous pearls shone resplendent in his shirt-front, and that he wore on his little finger a diamond solitaire of the finest water. The last item in this jeweller's window-display was a platinum bracelet which flashed with rubies, nestling half hidden in the forest on his wrist. At moments of extreme peril my sense of awareness sharpens to a fine point. At one and the same moment I noticed two things: that our box was being raked by the opera-glasses of a whole theatreful of society-people, all of them capable of the utmost ruthlessness in dealing with the less glorious members of their world, once they have gone off the rails: that this man, all hair and precious stones, had made a favourable impression on Florence. Gone were the days when she had taken the trouble to hold back. She as good as told him in so many words, even before he had kissed her hand, that all he need worry about was choosing the right moment and the right place. With boisterous good-humour Hourtinat accused me of not remembering him, and asked whether the ten years he had spent on a Gradignan farm had changed him 'all that much'. He had the presumption to sit down beside Florence and question her in an almost tender tone about her life in the country. He told us that local land-values had gone up nearly ten times, that the sale of resin was bringing him an almost fabulous return, as, too, was the turpentine which he was producing. His accent sounded quite frightful, even here, where the Sons of the great families, once they venture beyond the limits of the Department, produce a staggering effect on listeners every time they open their lips. I asked him, putting as much insolence as I could manage into my voice, whether he 'travelled' in diamonds. He greeted the question with a great guffaw of laughter which could be heard all over the theatre, and had the effect of putting an end to all conversation in our immediate neighbourhood.

'Values have gone all hay-wire,' he said: 'so, not knowing what to do with my money, I buy knick-knacks. Best investment you can make: but you haven't seen my really good stuff.'

Suddenly, he fished out of his waistcoat pocket a pinch of pearls which he spread—with considerable care—on the velvet ledge in front of Florence.

'Look at those, m'dear. They're what I give to the little ladies who take my fancy.'

The whole town had witnessed this incredible exhibition. I was on the point of showing him to the door when Florence's delighted laughter made me pause, though the man's terrific breadth of shoulder may also have had something to do with my hesitation. Consequently, it was I who made myself scarce. No sooner did they catch sight of me in the corridor than all the Castaingts, Duponts and Durands present crowded round me. I found, to my amazement, that the giant now installed in our box, had not only awakened their curiosity, but actually impressed them. What had set them off on the wrong scent was a vaguely negroid something in the handsome Hourtinat's face. I ought, perhaps, to mention that, in this part of the world, there is a good deal of active trading with our African colonies. The negro type is by no means frowned upon, for it quite often happens that those in whom it is visible may quite easily turn out to be related by blood to one or other of the great mercantile families whose 'bottoms' carry their fame and fortune all over the world. Since I had to do something to gain time, I assumed a somewhat mysterious air, and was careful not to deny even the most preposterous hypotheses advanced by the members of my audience. But would the prestige I had gained at this game prevent Hourtinat from, sooner or later, giving the lie to this legend—and, if so, how great would be my fall!

He saw us to the car, and invited us to lunch with him the next day at the *Panier fleuri*. Florence accepted before I had time to invent a prior engagement. I felt that I was lost. As we drove home, I heaped clumsy invectives on my sister's head. She pushed her cynicism to the point of saying that if I didn't want to turn up at lunch, she would be only too pleased to go alone, and would even be grateful to me for making it possible for her to do so. I should have felt less worried by this dig had I not known that since her marriage she had never failed to indulge her every curiosity.

I spent part of the night smoking and brooding in my book-lined study. How deeply shocked the Sons would have been had they discovered that the pages were actually cut! I blamed myself for having been so imprudent as to allow the Hourtinat legend to take root, since it would merely make the scandal the greater. The worst feature of the situation was that we had enemies. I tried to find comfort in the smallness of their number, but I knew that they were powerful—not only those rabid 'ultras' of the fashionable world who obstinately regarded us as upstarts, but also those old acquaintances whom we had 'dropped'. Ever since the war these had found a very convenient weapon to their hands which could be turned against the Maucoudinats. Up to 1914, that powerful family had gloried in the fact that old Madame Maucoudinat had been a Tanenbaum before her marriage. Though nothing here could take precedence of an English connexion, any name with a foreign sound produced a dazzling effect and marked its owner out for admiration in social circles. Now, however, Tanenbaum had an unfortunate sound, and produced a bad effect upon the lower orders. But why should I paint myself blacker than I am? On this particular night it was not only the man-of-the-world side of me that was calculating, in a mood of fear, the full total of our enemies. The brother in me, standing on the very edge of the abyss, was miserably, was desperately, trying to hold back his wretched sister from being the author of her own ruin.

IV

How well I remember that nightmarish luncheon in a famous restaurant. The ridiculous grottoes into which the town water-supply has been made to flow for the purpose of keeping gold-fish fresh and healthy, do nothing to relieve the suffocating atmosphere of the place. Scarcely more than five or six tables were occupied, and those by people who had come, as they might have come to a bawdy-house, with a single, clearly defined pleasure in view. I could hear the munching of truffles by strong and active jaws. The wine-waiter handled precious bottles with a sacramental air, and as cautiously as though they contained a charge of high-explosive. The faces of these gross feeders were deeply flushed, and the working of their jaws was clearly visible. Hourtinat left us in no doubt about what the *canard à l'orange*, the mush-rooms, the miraculous Médoc—and the pearl in his tie, had cost. Florence, well away after half a glass of Yquem, sat with her elbows on the table, gazing at him with an expression of sloppy approval. There was nothing to be hoped for from her amused sense of the ridiculous, especially in its more excessive manifestations. Her taste ran to extravagance in all things, and to clearly defined types of the human animal. To be sure, he had fine eyes, but can eyes ever really be called fine which see nothing of the world at large, find no enchantment in forms and colours, but are ever fixed with glassy intentness on their prey, whether it be a customer to cheat or a woman to strip? The fact of the matter is that Florence, completely detached from everything, was obsessed by a craving for the gutter—for her own utter degradation. Hourtinat asked for nothing better, and, quite obviously, never doubted that I should tactfully withdraw when the dessert appeared. Accustomed as he was to easy women, he wasn't going to put himself out for Florence who, in the time-table of his day, would be fitted in at half-past-three, after he had finished his cigar. Meanwhile, he displayed to what he took to be my admiring gaze, the plan of his new factory which he drew for my benefit on the table-cloth.

We left the restaurant. Hourtinat suggested a stroll along the quays 'just to settle the stomach'. He told me not to bother about him, but to hurry back to whatever it was I had to do. I said that I had nothing particular on hand. He was careful to walk on ahead with Florence, but I obstinately clung to their heels as they zig-zagged between the piles of hogsheads. We had to step over the bodies of sleeping dock-hands. A mist woven of sunbeams shrouded the yards and bows of ships at rest after their ploughing of the seas. Cranes, looking like tame elephants, were hoisting great packing-cases of sweet-smelling pine. Hourtinat had instructed his chauffeur to follow in the car at a discreet distance. In this way he had hoped to discourage my pursuit, but, all along the waterfront, the noble façade, on which venerable social maxims are inscribed in letters of gold, was a constant reminder of my duty. At last we reached the docks. Hourtinat was not the sort of man to go on doggedly playing a part in which he did not show to advantage. My determination not to yield an inch decided him to light a second cigar, which he did with a gesture which seemed to say: 'no hurry: no hurry at all.' Finally, his car came to my rescue. Florence addressed no word of reproach to me, but sat down on a bollard, and stared at the river.

I could contain myself no longer, I launched into a tirade

in the course of which I pointed out the risks she was running, and reminded her how, when we were children, we had been exposed to endless humiliations, and carried about with us the shameful knowledge that we belonged to a class of merchants whose business was not that of wine. I recalled the tricks and stratagems to which we had been reduced in later years, and our sense of triumph when her marriage had saved us from all that. She broke in on me to express the disgust she felt when she thought of all the plotting and scheming in which we had indulged. She said that her one unforgiveable crime had been to make use of Augustin (she called him the 'wonderful boy') in order to further our ambition to belong to the stupidest of all possible worlds. With painful violence she spoke of our lost friend. She reminded me of how he had looked at Sunday Vespers when she saw him from the gallery of the school chapel, ringed with solitude among the Sons of the Families—and then, at Gravette—a squalid little figure filled with contempt of all our pitiful social conventions.

'I exploited him just in order to marry a Maucoudinat, and he loved me! I asked nothing of him except to keep me amused by telling me the secrets of his birth and early life—and all that time, he loved me! . . . Loved me!'

'But you didn't love him, Florence. Don't you remember how you used to say that he was just a grubby, overgrown schoolboy, about whose father nobody knew anything, and that he turned your stomach. . . .'

'That's not true!'

'He turned your stomach even when you began to admire him, when he had already weaned you from all your thoughts of pride and precedence. . . .'

'What does it matter that I despised him then, if I love him now?'

Her voice was so loud that some men engaged in washing down the deck of one of the ships, stopped working, and stared at her with their hands shading their eyes. Gulls were swooping round the bows. In stormy weather they are carried inland, up the river. Out at sea the sky looked black.

I told Florence that this love of hers ought, at least, to preserve her from degrading adventures. She made no reply, and I pressed the point.

'What would Augustin have thought of that absurd Hourtinat!'

She burst out laughing:

'What he would really have despised would have been your terror at the thought of losing your position in the world of the "upper crust": the thought of Hourtinat in the middle of that cobweb society, laying about him and destroying its tiny labours, would merely have amused him.'

To this I replied that Augustin had had a longing for perfection, for renunciation. How completely master of himself that full-blooded young man had been! I had a feeling that this argument had got under my sister's defences, and I developed it with a crafty display of eloquence. I swore that her salvation was more important to me than anything else in the world, that I would gladly sacrifice my position among the Sons, provided *she* could be saved. As God is my witness, when I spoke those words I was utterly sincere. The hour of high-tide was approaching, and with it, as usual, a wind from the west. Lights began to show in an estaminet where foreign sailors sat drinking gin, whisky and schnapps. A heavily made-up woman in a wrap appeared at the door of a brothel. I put Florence's fur coat round her shoulders. Augustin, by teaching her to despise the world, had launched her on the road to perdition: could he not now bring her salvation by restoring to her a sense of inner beauty? . . . Perhaps . . . perhaps. . . . We got into a tram filled with exhausted workmen. Their eyes seemed abnormally large because of the coal-dust on their faces. One of them, seated on her right side, drew away to avoid touching her furs with his oil-stained sleeve. The voice in which she spoke to him had so much in it of goodness and simplicity, that I scarcely recognized it as hers. When we reached her door, I once again begged her to have nothing more to do with Hourtinat. To this she said nothing. I followed her up the stairs, still begging her to give me her word. She made a gesture which seemed to mean—him, or someone else, what does it matter? . . . We went into the small drawing-room where the only light came from a fire of pine-branches. It was then that, turning to me, she said:

'Only he can save me! You must bring Augustin back: you *must!*'

'But where can I find him, darling? He has been wandering about the world for twelve years, and we know nothing of him, not even whether he is still alive.'

She reminded me how Madame Etinger had said that during the first year of the war, she had sent him woollens, addressed to the Legion, but that he had never acknowledged them. I was on the point of saying—'How is it possible to go on believing that he isn't dead?'—but stopped myself just in time from committing so gross a blunder. I promised, instead, that I would bring our vanished friend back on condition that she showed Hourtinat the door. She jumped up, took both my hands in hers, and, almost in a whisper, said: '*Can* you do that? Can you?' Then, fearing that I might be making a fool of her, she said that she would give me a fortnight and no more in which to keep my promise. Her hair had come loose, and the look in her eyes was one of unrestrained supplication. Faced by that almost mad intensity, I suddenly hit upon a plan, and said, with complete confidence:

'In a fortnight from now, Florence, at this very hour, Augustin will be sitting opposite, and you will recognize him and will ask for his forgiveness.'

She laid a finger to her lips. A servant switched on the light, and showed in Madame Etinger.

All through that evening my sister thought only of making it easy for me to converse with Madame Etinger. Nothing in the world now mattered to her but that I should keep my word. She opened the piano so that I should be free to perfect my plans and make certain that Madame Etinger would be my ally. The good lady was very talkative, as she always was, when Maucoudinat was absent. She had a horror of him. She called him the 'chauffeur'—the 'ostler'. Harry Maucoudinat could not breathe in her rarefied atmosphere. He was not used to handling his inferiors with kid gloves, and laughed loudly when he should have sighed or shown emotion. But Madame Etinger had another, and more secret, reason for hating him. My brother-in-law had had the bad taste to make certain insinuations, which he regarded as humorous, about the excessive amount of work which Maître Balisac gave to Eva Etinger. That was the crime she could not overlook, and it played a great part in her passionate participation when she learned the nature of my plan. From the very first words I spoke, she was convinced that my sister and my friend had once been lovers. She was firm in her determination to keep on with me to the end. My denials had no effect upon her. It satisfied her hatred to think that Harry Maucoudinat had played second fiddle to Augustin, and that Eva was not the only forlorn young female capable of a romantic attachment. Meanwhile, I questioned her

on the subject of my friend's childhood, and it became clear
to me that, in spite of her exalted outlook, and the way she had
of seeing everything through the rosiest spectacles, she had
never really understood Augustin's greatness of mind. The
reason for this was that she was convinced of the necessity of
luxurious surroundings as a frame for refined feelings. What
she longed for was tragedy in which the protagonists should
behave like royalty and always dress for dinner.

'I have no idea what Augustin was like when he left school,
which was the period, I believe, at which your sister first
met him. No one could well have been grubbier than he was
as a child. It is true that he was left to the mercies of a venal
slut named Annette. Only someone with that vocation for
devotion, that love of sacrifice, which you know me to possess,
could have gone on frequenting that house at Clichy where his
unhappy father lived, surrounded by old papers and books,
busily occupied in editing a subversive magazine with the
help of wild and hairy men. But what a charmer he was!
When things were going well with him, and he was delivering
lectures on religious sensibility and the symbolism of dogma,
we were all mad about him! There was one young Polish girl,
whom I can see even now, with her hair worn low over a
prominent forehead like that of a Virgin, and her flax-blue
eyes, who went so far in her passionate devotion as to persuade
him to throw his doctorate to the winds! But about that time
he went over to the enemy, and the Polish girl had to have
their Augustin baptized in secret. . . . It was little short of heroic
on my part, sir, to remain faithful to them, and, several times
a week to share a meal with them not one scrap of which Eva
could touch. . . .'

With a vague look in her eyes, she nodded her head with
a compassionate smile which seemed to mean:—'I shall always

be incorrigible. My feelings are too strong for me. I just have to be sacrificed.' I asked her whether she had corresponded with Augustin's father up to the day of his death. She told me that the penitent, though he had never entered the Trappist Order, had lived in a strict retreat at Sept-Fonds, and that only ill-health had prevented him from taking the full monastic vows.

'But a barbarous director had forbidden him ever to see the child of his sin. I still have a deeply moving letter which I will show to you. In it he implored me to look after Augustin. It was very hard for me to send him no answer, and not to accede to his request. But Eva was exceptionally impression-able—it was the time when her character was being formed—and I did not wish her to be thrown into the boy's company, nor yet to breathe that morbid atmosphere. Besides, I am a religious woman and regularly fulfil the duties imposed upon me by my faith. Still, those Trappists sometimes observe a rigour of which I cannot approve. My conscience forbad me to be an accomplice in the abandonment to which they had condemned Augustin. That is why I never answered the letter, though, as you will see, it was imbued with much truly beauti-ful emotion. . . . Only God knows how much suffering it caused me. For a nature like mine, sacrifice means the assump-tion of an apparent hardness, an avoidance of that irresponsible charity to which I am prone. But that is how I am made.'

'But what about Augustin, madame?'

'As I have told you, he was a grubby little boy, who bit his nails to the quick, and always had some book or other bulging his pocket. He would bring a book to meals, and, since we were always at him, used to take refuge in the lavatory so as to be able to read his fill. I must confess that it passes my under-standing how he could ever have become a young man worthy of winning the approval of Madame Harry Maucoudinat.

But you may rely on me to bring him here on the appointed day. I like to think of him coming into this room and being introduced to your brother-in-law. . . .'

In these last words I found the explanation of her zealous co-operation. That Madame Etinger would ever be able to lay hands on my friend, as she said she could, seemed to me to be wholly illusory, the more so since she assumed an air of mystery. All I knew was that she was prepared to go into action on the very next day. I even had to advance her five hundred francs to cover the expenses of a journey the nature of which she wished to keep veiled in secrecy. I reminded her of the promise she had made to show me the letter written by Augustin's father. She said that I should have it that same evening, and she kept her word. But I did not read it at once because my mind was occupied with other matters. I had barely left her when I saw, more clearly than ever before, how little reliance I could place on her promises. How was it possible to doubt that from the month of August 1914 onwards, Augustin might have been killed a hundred times over? There was no reason to look for any other explanation of his silence. As to Madame Etinger, the prospect of travelling at my expense obviously appealed to her. Her daughter's relationship with Maître Balisac had reached a point of extreme delicacy, and the position was made the more difficult from her mother's being known far and wide as an idealist. One can go through life with one's head in the clouds without necessarily coming to grief: all the same, the best way of avoiding certain contingencies, is to take a train. It was, therefore, very right and proper that Madame Etinger should take a little trip and enjoy a change of scene, but not for one moment did I really believe that she would find our friend. My scepticism was strengthened when, for several days after her departure, not so much as a postcard reached me. As the result of an enquiry made by one of our Paris customers at the War Ministry, it transpired that two men with the name of Augustin had been reported missing.

Meanwhile, Florence waited. She spent most of the day in a chair, doing nothing but stare at the door, and the wild look in her eyes might well have given the impression that she was mad, had she not, thank God, given instructions to the servants to say that she was at home to nobody. Hourtinat plied the knocker in vain. The gossip to which his appearance in our box had given rise, was beginning to die down. It was not, however, true to say that my sister never thought of him. When the butler one day said to her in my presence: 'Monsieur Hourtinat asks me to say that he must have a word with madame'—I could see that she was waging a battle against her instinctive desires, that she was the victim of an insidious temptation. The ghost of Augustin was not always a strong enough defence against a man who, only too obviously, had a flesh and blood existence. Nevertheless, she did continue to put up a successful resistance, and I should have been in the seventh heaven had I not realized that, sooner rather than later, I should be inevitably forced to show results. My sister was in a state of almost mystical exaltation. She no longer entertained the faintest doubt of my success, and, on more than one occasion, quite gratuitously informed me of her intention of wearing in Augustin's honour, and in spite of the unsuitability of the season, a white linen dress of the kind that had been fashionable in that blazing August of long ago at Gravette, when he had been in love with her. I feared the worst, for her disillusionment would be so terrible that it might well disturb her mental balance. In any case, I knew my sister too well not to realize that disappointment would almost certainly make her use such sanity as she had left in revenging herself upon me, and that in a way which would touch me on the raw. I trembled to think that, in a week's time, she might be publicly flaunting her relationship with Hourtinat, or someone like him. It was a sure thing that the Sons would never permit one of their number to be made a fool of by a rustic clod, and that Harry Maucoudinat would no longer be kept in that condition of blissful ignorance of which only his peers could be allowed to enjoy the fruits. Consequently, I reverted to the idea which, at first, I had thought so wonderful when I had made up my mind to delude Florence with an absurd hope. That idea had, at the time, been utterly senseless, but now, seeing the state of unbalance in which she was, her air of living in a constant condition of somnambulism, I persuaded myself that even the crudest trap would catch her. After all, what risk did I run? Briefly, my plan was to make full use of Jean Queyries' physical likeness to Augustin, which was so staggering that it alone had been sufficient to make me find his companionship delightful.

In a few moments Jean Queyries will be with me. How can I make that very down-to-earth young man understand what it is that I require of him? Even if he does, is it likely, that he will be willing to face the fact that he is not to be loved for himself, that in him Florence will be seeing a beloved rival? But lovers are strange creatures, and it may be that he will take the bait. I regard him as a young man with an eye to the main chance, whose feet are firmly planted on the ground. He is one of those, or so I have always thought; who confound love with ambition. What he is chiefly after is to gain admittance to our 'world', even if he can do so only by the back-door. What I have to do is to coach him in his part, and the only danger I can see will come from Florence who may reveal the trick. I can hear a footstep in the street. It is Jean's. He will be here in a minute.

V

22nd February: midnight

I FIND that I have never really known Jean Queyries at all, or, rather, that I have never taken the trouble to know him. When he used to drop in of an evening, what I liked was to go on looking at him while all the time thinking of somebody else. To see his face was happiness enough for me, and I paid little attention to what he said. Only as the result of what happened the other night have I discovered that he belongs to the race of those precocious Don Juans, whose characteristics I shall now amuse myself by describing. This will be the easier for me to do since, so long as Florence believes that I am running about the country in search of Augustin, I am careful to spend as much time as possible in my study, where I find writing a great distraction. Let me begin by saying that he entered wholeheartedly into my scheme, and was not in the least embarrassed by my somewhat obscure explanations. Naturally enough, I told him only what it was impossible for me to conceal. The picture of Florence which I painted for his benefit was that of a sick woman obsessed by the memory of a childhood's friend, and I managed to convince him that the doctor, worried lest her neurasthenic condition might grow worse, wanted to find some way of persuading her that the friend is still alive.

'It so happens, my dear Jean, that you bear a curious

resemblance to this Augustin, who was exactly the same age as you are now when he left us ten years ago.'

He pointed out to me that ten years can make a lot of difference, and that Madame Maucoudinat would find it difficult to understand how her friend, seen again after so long an interval, could still be looking like a young man. I assured him that my sister was living in a dream world, the prey to a dreadful illusion, and would be very easily taken in.

No sign of emotion showed in his face as, in measured tones, he reviewed a number of hypotheses. I could see at once that he has a very considerable knowledge of women, though he lacks all trace of culture. He is a little middle-class type with those factual tendencies which he seems to share with most of the young people of to-day who have never read *Les Liaisons dangereuses*, *Adolphe*, or *Volupté*. He has no idea who *Julien Sorel* is, nor *Fabrice del Dongo*, and has never so much as heard of *Emma Bovary* or *Madame Arnoux*. Of the two of us, however, it was I who appeared to be the ignoramus. Apparently one learns more about passion in a discreet basement room than from books. My literary knowledge, however, and his experiences seem to have led us to much the same conclusions. It is people like me whom reading has released from the necessity of living, while living has released Jean Queyries from the necessity of reading those analyses of an inclination which he spends every day in satisfying. Since he puts forward no claim to be a philosopher, it never occurs to him that the affairs in which he indulges can have any importance. Jean is not one of those whom a passionate word or a caress can bind for eternity.

25th February, eleven a.m.

From the confidences with which he has honoured me, the

questions that he has put to me about Florence, and his descriptions of the strokes of luck which have come his way, I have got a pretty clear idea that a boy of his type, though not fundamentally bad, is unlikely to be capable of pity. Fully aware of his own youthful attractions, he knows that, in spite of inevitable rupture and eventual abandonment, any woman with whom he finds his passing pleasure owes the happiest moments of her life to him, and that none of those whom he has quite frankly deserted would wish that what had happened between them had never been. Jean is sufficiently artless to admit that, no matter what the future may be for them, the ephemeral women in his life all, in the long run, say 'thank you'. He gives himself to many who make the running—that is his social function—and when, after the breach, he says—'What have they got to complain about, they've had their fun, haven't they?'—one senses in him the self-satisfaction of the male who has done his duty.

I did not even have to 'explain' Florence to him. Ever since he started looking at her from a distance, watching her with the concentrated patience of a cat, he has realized that there is nothing about her character that he does not know already. I shall have my work cut out if I start trying to make use of this young gentleman. What I want is for him to save her, but shall I be able to keep the young hound to heel, and teach him not to go hunting for his own sake? What I have got to do is find a good strong collar: I must do something about that. Still, the fact remains that I am playing a dangerous game, and am engaged in a pretty unsavoury adventure! Jean, who has a facile impudence, does not for a moment doubt that he will succeed in his attempt. I did my best to impress upon him that what is at issue is something a great deal more serious than a happy ending to his amorous enterprise, but should have despaired of making any impression had not an unexpected side of his nature been revealed to me. It is a trait he has in common with a number of gigolos, of the kind, I mean, who are attracted by the stage. So delighted are they with their own good looks that they long to exhibit themselves behind the foot-lights, and to become the idols of the mob. These narcissistic young fellows rapidly reach a point at which they can no longer rest content with a few private love-affairs. They dream of a collective adoration addressed to them by the public and, away from the theatre, feel that they are hiding their light under a bushel. Jean Queyries, in spite of his tremendous social ambitions, has kept up his membership of a boys' club, simply and solely because it enables him to do a bit of play-acting. Vocation, with him, has got the better of snobbery. Actually, though his technique is absurdly bad, he is not without a certain gift for the drama. I realized this when I asked him to read aloud some of Augustin's favourite poets. I was tickling his actor's vanity, and challenging him to give a natural rendering of Augustin whom, in fundamentals, he so little resembles. He was on his mettle at once, and I must confess that I found the result amazing. Perhaps professionals in love are born actors as well as born lovers. They excel in such matters as vocal modulation, and can ring the changes on their personalities according as they are called upon to wheedle a lady, a lady's-maid, a working-woman, or a girl with religious leanings. . . . Debauchery is a school in which a man learns how to know the hearts of many differing types. But Jean has got to play up to Florence for a good deal longer than the few hours taken by a stage performance. Once Hourtinat is out of the way, will he be able to maintain the lyric note? It is quite possible that Florence may help him to do so, though it is also possible that he may induce her to embark upon a few practical experiments. I don't very much care if he does, so long as they remain secret. Why should I feel scruples about landing Florence in *one* love affair provided it keeps her out of a hundred-thousand? The pseudo-Augustin will draw a *cordon sanitaire* round her, and keep her from the attentions of unworthy gallants. But if the programme does contain a few tumblings not envisaged in the terms of our agreement, I have no doubt that Jean will give them a certain air of sublimity. He comes here very often to rehearse his part as miracle-monger. The mystery in which the whole business is wrapped amuses him, but I rather dread his lack of discretion. I do not feel at all sure that he may not turn out to be the sort of cock who loudly announces the news of victory before the battle has been joined, and counts his chickens before they are hatched. I have decided to buy his silence by offering to introduce him into our world. He is wildly anxious to achieve that consummation. He would not be a native of this town if that sort of investiture did not seem to him all that really matters. I wonder what he thinks of me? It is pretty obvious that he is on the watch. Whether he accepts the reasons I have given him for this little plot of mine, I do not know, but I feel pretty sure he realizes that more than my sister's health is at stake. He said the other day, quite casually, that he couldn't understand why I was so worked up. Thank God, it never occurs to him that Madame Harry Maucoudinat's brother could possibly be worried about his own position in the world of society.

'I believe you're bored'—he said—'and all this mystification amuses you.'

It is true that, over and above my practical anxieties, there is something else, something amounting almost to anguish, that keeps me in a state of uneasy alertness: I am looking for an alibi.

Soon, the breathing-space allowed me by Florence will be over. I know that I shall have to beat a retreat, and it entertains me to ponder over this strange concatenation of circumstances. I find myself wondering at the mingled grandeur and pettiness that they contain. A petty desire to maintain our position in the world of Big Business has set me plotting and trifling with the chimaeras of Florence's mind, and the obscure passions of her heart. Formerly, we made use of Augustin to force the doors of that world—and now, here am I again making use of him at a time when, beyond all possible doubt, he has departed this life. It is a morning of sunlight and mist. A salty smell is coming off the river which the ocean tides have set moving. The sirens of the tugs, the clanging of the trams, the curses of lorry-drivers, come up to me as from another planet. . . . How odd it is that so mediocre a passion as vanity should stir in someone else the most romantic of passions. . . . But no! If, from where you are now, Augustin, you can read my heart, you must know that I am misrepresenting myself; that nothing in me is so strong at this moment as a desire to save that same Florence who long ago aroused in you so sad a love.

VI

26th February

No! I am not going through with this. I rang up Jean Queyries at his office meaning to tell him to forget everything we had planned. He was out when I telephoned him, but I expect him this evening. Will he submit without a struggle? How could I ever have brought myself to conceive so base a piece of deception, even to save Florence? How is it that some part of myself didn't rise in protest? Oh, my town, you must indeed have caught and ensnared me, paralysed me with your customs! This is where all my cunning diplomacy, my knowledge of men, has landed me! Neither reason nor conscience have sounded a word of warning. If now, at the very last moment, I am slipping from under, no credit is due to me, for I owe this eleventh hour decision to somebody now dead, to somebody I never knew;—to Augustin's father.

I had put off reading the unhappy man's letter which Madame Etinger, true to her promise, confided to me. Yesterday evening, after leaving the club, where I had been conscious of a slight coldness on the part of the Sons, of a sort of reticence hard to define, I came home in a gloomy mood. There is nothing worse, after a battle has been joined, than that moment of inaction when the die has been cast. I sat down at my table and opened and shut one book after another. No fiction had any power over my obsessive thoughts, nor could those

thoughts free me from the weight of a terrible boredom, or
overcome the sense of self-disgust from which I was suffering.
Then, I remembered the letter, and turned to it for distraction.
All I asked of it was to keep my mind off other things.

Even before I began to puzzle out the writing, which zig-
zagged across the paper from top to bottom like forked
lightning, I felt a pang of emotion when I saw the half-erased
date and heading: *Septfons: 12th February*, 190 . . . I shut my eyes.
I tried to summon up a picture of two boys, Augustin and me,
as we had sat that year at evening prep, with the heat making
our chilblains itch. The mist on the window-panes made it
impossible for us to see anything outside except the wild
waving of a plane-tree in the cold darkness. I shall not transcribe
here even the more intelligible passages in the letter: every so
often the thread of thought is broken by ejaculations, by allu-
sions to incidents I know nothing of. What the poor man is
trying to do in it is to get a promise from Madame Etinger
that she will look after Augustin. No doubt, when he wrote,
he was fully aware of that lady's idealistic attitude, for it is
only too apparent that he was terrified that she might turn a deaf
ear to his appeal. This I gathered from the endless and confused
arguments, many of which I have failed to follow. I had to
study the letter like a palimpsest in order to extract from it the
story which, when I had read it, touched me to the heart,
awoke in me a sense of remorse, a tardy feeling of shame, and,
at long last this paltry little determination to undo, as far as
possible, what I have done.

Augustin's father first describes to Madame Etinger the
long paved passage on to which, at Septfons, the cells of the
retreatants open, and where, he says, he has remained for a
long while, stunned and motionless after an interview with the
Prior. When, seeking mercy, he had fallen exhausted at the

door of that Trappist monastery, he had believed that he was prepared to accept no matter what penance, feeling that no burden would be too heavy for him to bear. But the horrible sentence passed upon him had kept him rooted to the spot. He had been told that he must never again set eyes on his illegitimate child. He was promised that everything possible should be done to see that the boy should not be neglected, that provision should be made for his needs. He had been assured, solemnly, and as though from the very lips of the Lord, that nothing could be of more effective assistance to Augustin, in this world and the next, than this sacrifice. Madame de Lavallière, when she became a penitent, expressed the wish that her son's name should never be mentioned in her hearing. Was he, then, to show himself less strong than that notorious light-o'-love? In his very first words the Prior had mentioned the one penance which, to Augustin's father, seemed more wicked than his crime. For a long time the wretched man wrestled with himself; that evening, when the gentle *Salve Regina* rose from the heart of darkness to the vaulted roof; all through the nightly Office, when sleep and cold are in league against the passionate will to achieve the proper state of self-communion, and, finally, at the early morning Mass, when each man, dressed in white, walks slowly back after receiving the Sacrament, matching his pace with that of the friend beside him, with his arm resting on his shoulder. When the sun rose, he knew that he was beaten, and sped away like a thief. He could not remember how he had reached a distant railway-station. That night he crossed Paris. 'After those days spent in retreat'—he writes—'the posters on walls and palisades, had the effect upon me of deafening cries.' Another train took him to the town where Augustin was living. He left the station before the first trams had mingled their lighted windows with the glimmer of the early dawn. A baker in whose shop he ate a morsel of bread hot from the oven, directed him to the school —his road to Calvary, an ill-defined and muddy thoroughfare, lined with one-storey houses under the despairing suburban sky where the day is brought to birth in pain.

At the school-gate he took stock of himself and saw that he looked like a tramp. Could he appear before his son in such a state? Augustin, it is true, had never known him in the days of his well-ordered, his almost glorious, life, could remember only the accursed home where his father had fought against the renewed and furious grappling of the faith which, hated and rejected, had again become exigent and dominating. It was bad enough that he should still retain the image of his father as he had been then! But that image was, at least, now half effaced, was softened and confused in outline. It must not be supplanted by another so nightmarish that it would remain with him as an obsession for the rest of his life. . . . Meanwhile, he had skirted the wall of the park. Where its place was taken by an old fence of black and rotting wood, he passed through. Clumps of evergreen concealed him. Copses hid on every side the playgrounds from which there reached his ears the birdlike cries of boys released for the morning break. He forced his way forward towards those cries with which his silent son must not mingle his own. Moving from tree to tree, each wreathed in mist, he drew closer. But the mist had reduced all human figures to mere shadows. Since most of the boys were playing at the further end of the yard, he hoped that his son might have been attracted to this quiet corner on the confines of the park. He could not believe that this harsh pleasure would be withheld from him, and, within himself, a silent cry burst forth—'I am thirsty, thirsty for this presence which is more bitter to me than the sponge soaked in vinegar!'—and then, suddenly, he saw him—a lonely boy coming in his direction. There was a smear of ink upon the broad and splendid brow. Two hands, swollen with chilblains, gripped the railing. The mist, by this time, had turned to a cold rain, and the boy pulled over his head a hood which, no doubt, some of his mischievous companions had filled with stones and earth, for his hair was covered in muck, and from some invisible group of onlookers came shouted gibes and guffaws of laughter. He did not so much as turn his head, but unfastening the cape with stiff, swollen fingers, gave it a shake and then put it on again. His skinny shoulders were shivering: the hood hid all of his face except the mouth. Then, did Augustin's father stretch his arms out to the boy: it was all he had time to do, for, just as he was about to follow up the gesture by running forward and embracing his son, a bell suddenly rang. At once the urchins stopped their noise and the playground sucked in the whole crowd of them. A moment later it was no more than an empty stage when the curtain has fallen. The boy was the last to move, and walked so slowly that his father could watch him melt and vanish into the mists of eternity. The sound of a master's voice came to him:

'Late as usual, Augustin. I believe you do it on purpose. No one-o'clock break for you: I shall keep you in.'

I find it difficult to understand how the father could have stopped himself from intervening between the boy and his tormentors. This part of the letter is confused and confusing. I can only assume that he acted as he did in obedience to some inner warning that his appearance on the scene would have injured, rather than helped, Augustin; that he was responding to some sort of conviction that only by renouncing his son could he save him. . . . To put forward so mystical an explanation of his behaviour was the last thing he would have done if he still had any hope that he might influence Madame Etinger in his favour. She can scarcely have failed, however, to respond to such an ejaculation as—'Renunciation is something that I must endlessly renew. No vow can be taken just once and for all and left at that. Not for a single second must the knife be lifted from the throat.' The pious nonsense with which the poor man's letter ends makes it easy to understand how he could have become an arch-heretic. It had not been because he had any leanings to rationalism, but, rather, that he displayed an only too reckless faith in inspiration and interior revelation, in what is called religious experience. This craving for the sensible marks of Grace betrays a sensual temperament carried to excess. The reading of these ravings had the effect of restoring my composure. No tears flowed. Since when had I lost the gift of tears? Perhaps since the day when, still a schoolboy, Augustin taught me the prayer he ranked above all prayers: '*Almighty and most merciful God, who didst bring forth living water from the rock that the thirst of Thy people might be slaked, bring forth now from the hardness of our hearts tears of compunction. . . .*'

But all within me is not rottenness. I cheated Augustin in his lifetime, but I will not do so now that he has left this world. I will not make use of him to further my imbecile passion: I will not involve that pure and vanished spirit in the dirty processes of social snobbery and loose adultery. Blessed, thrice-blessed is the letter which has checked me at the very moment when I was on the point of acquiescing in so gross an infamy. I want to spend this sad and silent evening in your company, Augustin: the hours of this night I will dedicate to our dear memories. You shall help me to achieve that solemn examination of my conscience as a result of which I hope to be born again as I was in the days when you loved me. Beyond time and space we have been re-united: we can do no more than

can the stars to fight against this meeting. Together we are
gravitating. . . .

Somebody has rung my bell. Can it be Jean Queyries
already? With what feelings of joy shall I set about destroying
the work of my hands and breaking, one by one, the meshes
of the net which I have stretched!

VII

Same evening

IDNIGHT. The wretched creature has gone, but all my ashtrays are still smoking from the accumulated butts of his cigarettes. When I saw, not Jean Queyries at my door, but Percy Larousselle in full evening-dress, with that arrogant monocle stuck in his face, and the look of a man who has got more aboard than he can carry, I knew that I was in for trouble. Ever since Florence sent him packing, he has hated us. How could I have been such a fool as not to foresee that he would get his blow in first? It needed only a glance for me to realize—like a man taken by surprise who is quick to notice the knife in his attacker's hand—that Percy had carried the war into my own country. He called me 'old man', asked how things were with me, while, all the time, he was looking for the vital spot at which to strike. Half sitting on, half leaning against, my table, he dangled one of his pumps on a silk-clad toe. After an interval of silence he opened his mouth, and I braced myself for the blow.

'Not dressed yet, old man?'

When I told him that I was going nowhere that evening, he expressed surprise that I shouldn't be looking in on the James Castaingt ball.

'Is it to-night?'

I had got to my feet, amazed that I should have forgotten all about so outstanding a social event. I was so entirely occupied, thanks to Florence, Jean Queyries and Augustin, with living in the past and the future, that I had no time left for the formidable present. Fully aware of the blunder I was committing (it was too late for me to parry the thrust) I stammered something about it's being incredible that I should have received no card. Percy's grin of triumph stretched his face so wide that the monocle fell out of his eye-socket. Nevertheless, he pretended astonishment. Did I really mean to say I hadn't been invited? What an extraordinary thing!—probably lost in the post.

'Of course the company'll be pretty select: you know how choosy the James Castaingts are. Still, there must have been a mistake—I expect somebody forgot to post the invitation: would you like me to telephone, just to get the mystery cleared up?'

His drunkard's hand trembled for a moment above the instrument. Then, with a sudden change of mind, he started muttering, like somebody just remembering something:

'Half a mo—yes, it's all coming back to me . . . yes, I've got it, old man . . . piece of pure misunderstanding, that's all it was . . . they were talking about it at the club the other day, something to do with a chap called Hourtinat . . .'

At that I completely lost my head: 'My sister has never had anything to do with Hourtinat!'—I shouted. The man, he told me, had been seen hanging about of an evening under Florence's windows. Their relationship was the talk of the place. I was pretty near crying, and, ass that I was, played into the enemy's hands. He made a fine pretence of pulling up short—ought never, he said, to have passed that piece of gossip on—mustn't let it worry me. . . . Then, he added:

'All things considered, I think I *won't* ring up . . . much better, believe me, to leave stories like that alone. I'd be only too glad to exchange places with you: God knows, *I* don't want to hang around at that ball. Why not let's all meet later at the *Lion rouge*?—Olympe, Marcelle and Carmen'll be there. Wait till we turn up, old man, and I'll tell you how it went.'

He moved to the side-table where there was a decanter of port and filled his glass twice in quick succession, thereby giving me the chance to rally my forces. I assumed a careless air, and pointed out that they all knew how much I detested dancing. I had said as much, more than once, in the hearing of the James Castaingts. Good friends that they were, they had been afraid of plaguing me, though I was rather sorry that they had taken me at my word. Percy, whose reading had not taught him subtlety, also took me at my word. The fool thought it the best way of reassuring me, but so afraid was he of being cheated of his revenge and burning his boats, that he said suddenly:

'But why didn't they ask your sister?—they know she loves dancing.'

With the obstinacy of a drunken man, he stuck to his point:

'If anyone loves dancing she does: you must admit that.'

Once again the port-decanter exerted its fascination. Notwithstanding his evening-dress, he was exactly like one of the men who haunt the bars down by the harbour, standing at the counter and drinking. He had just their way of emptying a glass at one go. The only difference between them was that he had not worn himself out by hoisting bales and sacks all day. His house was very different from the hovels where emaciated children swarmed round bitter-tongued and ageless women. He put the empty decanter back on the table, and, swaying on his feet, said:

'*We've* led that Florence of yours a dance . . . the whole bloody lot of us! . . .'

He began to chuckle. Ash from his cigarette was on his shirt-front. A sudden spurt of anger, uncontrollable but lucid, brought me to my feet. I remembered how once, when he was cold sober, he had knocked out a couple of dockers, but, in the state he was now, the tiniest David could have had him grovelling. So, I went for him. In a blind fury I gripped his two forearms. His crush-hat rolled on the floor. It needed only a push to send him crashing backwards on to the divan. I showered blows on him, breaking his monocle and cutting my right hand. The sight of blood steadied me. Sobered all of a sudden, he scrambled to his feet. Not a word did he utter. With a single bound I went to earth behind the table, and took a revolver from the drawer. Percy Larousselle's face was livid. A circular bruise showed round his eye where the monocle had been. It was not on the shoulder that society had branded this gaol-bird. He stammered out:

'My seconds will call on you tomorrow! . . . I'll kill you like a dog . . . like a dog!'

There was something feeble in the way he made the threat. I don't think he wanted to have this incident publicized. Oddly, though I had never held a foil in my life, and knew that Percy was a practised swordsman, the thought of death did not enter my mind at that moment: all I was concerned about was my knowledge that this duel would be the end of me, socially speaking, that it would set the seal on my downfall. I went through the pretence of laughing: was this all the thanks I got for sobering him?—I asked: when dealing with a drunk a few good punches could do wonders.

Experienced swimmers, when they have to do a bit of life-saving always begin by stunning the drowning man. That was why I had gone for him. Of course, if he was still determined to fight. . . . It was obvious to me that Percy was not taken in, but also, that he wanted nothing better than to find a way of wriggling out, and I was giving him one. Suddenly, he exclaimed:

'My stud!—God almighty, where's my pearl stud got to!'

He went down on his hands and knees. His spread coat-tails made him look ridiculous. It was I who found the pearl, behind the divan. He thanked me, and apologized for having taken our little set-to so seriously. But even while he was speaking words of peace I could see by the look in his eyes that he was determined to bring me down. He said:

'You meant well, and I've no hard feelings: only, you might have treated my dress-suit a bit more gently: put me back two thousand at Guarigue's, I'd have you know. Can you lend me a clean shirt and collar—I don't want to have to go home. It's the least you can do!'

How cordial and friendly he was! But I knew just how much —or how little—it meant. Still, I did everything I could to help, so pleased was I that matters hadn't turned out worse. While he was tidying himself up in my bedroom, I sat in solitude hearing the horns of cars on their way to the house of James Castaingt, which would be blazing with lights, like so many moths fluttering to the flame. The letter written by my friend's father still lay on the table. The feelings it had aroused such a short time before were still working in me, but I was in the grip of a savage longing to triumph a second time over the Sons. I knew now that I should play out my little game to the end. All the same, I was perfectly clear-headed. I harboured no illusions about Florence. She was beyond all help, and I knew that I should never succeed in leading her into the way I wanted her to follow. There was a pride in her outrageousness which left no room for calculation and trickery. What saves so many women from destruction is their very baseness, their cowards' caution and mean strategies. But true profligacy and vice demands a hideous sort of courage which cares nothing about social taboos. Florence was floundering in deep waters. All the same, I would try my luck.

Percy came back into the study. He was holding one of my collars in his hand, and grumbling. It was too small for him, he said. He asked for half-a-glass of salad-oil which, according to him, is a sovereign cure for a hang-over. Then he stretched himself out on the divan where, such a short time ago, I had been pummelling him, saying that he would take a short nap to get himself into better shape. Only a few seconds elapsed before the disgusting creature was snoring. In the half-light his dissipated face looked emaciated, as though worn thin by spiritual torment. In sleep, perhaps, his vices crept away, for now, on those relaxed features, no trace of them remained. As happens when one rubs a coin clean, the effigy emerges clear and bright, so did his youth show suddenly fresh and unsullied. I was reminded of that now so distant afternoon when Florence and I had watched the sleeping Augustin whom already I was betraying.

VIII

THIS is the last evening before I shall have to foot the inevitable bill, and I have been spending it with my sister. She believes that I have just got back from a difficult and exhausting trip. I did not wait until we had exchanged greetings, but said at once:

'He will be here tomorrow.'

She showed no astonishment. She had not doubted for a single moment that I should bring Augustin back, but she asked me on a note of deep concern:

'How is he?'

I realized that she was less concerned with Augustin's health than his appearance. How would that face look after the experiences of these last years, all of them sharper and more rending than briars? Her question led me to think that she was, perhaps, rather less unaware of what was going on than I had supposed. I gave myself a pat on the back for not having listened to the argument put forward by Jean Queyries, who had wanted me not to see Florence before he made his entry. 'It's most important,' he had said, 'for her to be on tenterhooks up to the very last moment.' But he had failed to convince me.

The afternoon on which he and I met to put the finishing touches on this precious piece of impersonation, was a painful experience. I professed to feel uneasiness on the ground of my sister's neuraesthenia, and expressed regret that it had compelled me to have recourse to so much double-dealing. At this qualm of mine Jean merely smiled. He was no longer even pretending to be taken in. He asked me about the Castaingt ball, but in so detached a way, that I found his curiosity offensive. Was our downfall already the common gossip of the lower elements in the town? I knew, too, that Percy Larousselle had not been inventing when he had talked about Hourtinat's self-imposed sentry-duty under Florence's windows. Had things really gone no further between besieger and besieged? I did not want to believe the current tittle-tattle; but Florence's air of despondency earlier in the evening, the remorse which I thought I could read in her face, made me think that, perhaps, she was being yielding, imprudent. . . . How weak is the flesh, how utterly defenceless!

Could Jean Queyries really manage to keep at bay the many Hourtinats now prowling round her? Above all, could he maintain his miserable partner for long in the rarefied climate of an emotion at once passionate and chaste? I must, I felt, put this delicate point into words. I pretended that I doubted his ability to give to his love that final gloss of purity, that seeming thirst for perfection which had meant so much in Augustin's power to charm. Jean, like so many of the young men who are in love with their own good looks and dream of the stage, deeply resented having his talent for playing different parts convincingly, called in question.

'I can do Polyeucte just as well as Nero'—he said: 'when I was fifteen I played both at the boys' club, and had a big success.'

'I don't doubt that'—I said jokingly: 'Polyeucte escaping martyrdom by a miracle, and with something of Grace stripped from him, finding Pauline married to Severus—for that is precisely what you have got to be.'

He seemed to catch my meaning. I am expecting a great deal of him. It is Florence I am frightened about.

This evening, after putting that question to me—'How is he?'
—she once more sat down in front of a meagre fire. After a few
deceptively fine days, the bad weather had returned, and was
lashing at the windows. She was still in her dressing-gown,
and, with her carelessly pinned-up hair looked as though she
had just got out of bed. The only sound to be heard was the
droning voice of Eliane on the floor above, learning a story.
It was then that, with infinite precaution, I described Augustin
to her. He looked very different, I said, from the boy we had
known, though he still had an air of youth which time seemed
powerless to change. She listened to me without the least
appearance of surprise. Old age, she replied, is a form of evil,
and the passage of the years wears out the body far less than do
our actions.

'His purity has kept him from growing old. But what about
me? Is not the whole of my life visible on my face?'

Words, she believed, were unnecessary, for does not the
mere look of our sad and wasted bodies make full confession?
To this I answered that youth can make our vices tolerable,
that borne upon its waves the most hideous monsters can take
on a beauty of reflected colouring. But once the years of youth
are gone, the shores of our life are strewn with flaccid jellyfish.
. . . Because she was seated at some distance from the lamp, I
could not clearly see her face. She may not have been crying,
but there came from her an emanation of infinite despair. I
could find no words of comfort when she said:

'Nothing can wash us clean—nothing! nothing!'

Doubtless, though she did not know it, she was hoping that
I would protest. She went on:

'And nothing can remit our sins.'

She said no more, but sat waiting for the words I could not
utter. It is at such moments that, in the presence of one dying of

thirst, though we know his need of water, we cannot find a vessel in which to collect it, and are, in any case, too far from the wells in which the water sleeps. We do not know the roads that lead to them, and, if we did, they are too long and steep for legs to negotiate that are stiff from long enslavement to the things of this world. That was why I said nothing.

The fire crackled: the moan of sirens from the harbour reached our ears through the sound of wind and falling rain. Florence stretched her hands fanlike to the flames. I owe it to myself to say that in those moments of deep distress, her salvation was all that mattered to me—her salvation and not my own social position. What lie has ever served to draw a soul up from perdition? Yet, with infinite patience, I now plunged into a lie.

'Only Augustin, darling, can absolve you. He has come back from the past to save you. From the buried years of our youth he has returned to you. He will ask no questions, but his mere presence will wipe out from the pages of your past all that has been written there since he went away. Remember, Augustin had only to tell you his story, there, beside the sea, for your heart to be renewed.'

In a low, weak voice, Florence said:

'Yes . . . yes . . .'

'Don't you believe me, Florence?'

In scarcely more than a whisper, she replied:

'I am afraid of myself.'

She covered her face with her two hands. The gesture was eloquent of shame. Gently, I pulled them apart, and touched her forehead with my lips.

IX

Piraillon, on the shore of the Gravette inlet. May, 192 . . .

AFTER an interval of several weeks, I have been going through the senotes, amazed to find that the writing is my own. It was I that wrote them, but to-day I am a different person. Through the plank walls of a fisherman's hut I can hear upon the sand the swish and rustle of warm, soft, summer waves, like the sound of dead leaves. How close that sound seems—like a voice at my ear. Perhaps the water is splashing the door and the stone of its threshold. In just such a way, when I was a young boy, did I lie in bed, my heart attuned to the movement of the stars, listening to the flowing tide. The night is filled with the silence of the worlds: meteors flash and fall without a sound, and the Great Bear makes no more noise than a cicada. What am I doing here?—what can I try to do except overcome my repugnance at the thought of what has happened?

At five o'clock on a Saturday afternoon, Florence was waiting for me to keep my promise, for Augustin to come. At four, Jean had been shown into my study. The first thing I noticed was that he had not carried out as closely as I could have wished the instructions I had given him about his general get-up. To be sure, he was wearing a working coat with shiny elbows and a blue flannel shirt, but, in spite of these concessions, anyone who had remembered Augustin's squalid appearance in the old days, would have found his air of elegance rather too excessive. His youthfulness, too, worried me. Even allowing for her dreamlike state, could I really believe that Florence would be so far deceived as to accept the fact that ten years had passed without in any way impairing the freshness of that face? I tried to find comfort in the thought that when she had first known Augustin she had fallen a victim to his personality without being at all in love with him. It was only in the course of years that she had grown to be passionately attached to the image of him which she kept stored away in her memory, and embellished at leisure, an image so completely idealized that no reality could ever efface it. All the same, I did insist on Jean ruffling his hair. I also made him break the laces of his shoes and tie them together again in an untidy knot. The young man obeyed, but with a bad grace. Though he was afraid of displeasing me, and made a rebellious effort to satisfy my whims, it hurt his pride to appear shabby in the eyes of the woman whom he was hoping to dazzle. He had not my reasons for wishing to pass for another, and was well aware that even with the most delicate-minded of young women quite crude things, like the cut of a man's coat, do matter. Besides, through Florence the cooper's son hoped to gain entry into the world of Big Business, and didn't think that he could do that in a flannel shirt and with shiny elbows. In well-chosen words I warned him not to misuse his victory. Florence, I said, would introduce him to our friends, but only on condition that he did not parade her as his property. In that way I unmasked a few of my batteries. He understood perfectly well that what I wanted was that he should create round Florence an atmosphere of passion through which no Hourtinat would ever be able to penetrate. I let him believe that he could rely upon my tolerance, even upon my complicity, so long as he kept their intrigue a secret. 'This resemblance you have to Augustin can, if you wish it, give an appearance of nobility, of purity to your love. But I don't want to have to shut my eyes, Jean. What matters is that there should be nothing for me to see, that, thanks to you Florence, made happy, shall never again be an object of gossip. Do you understand what I mean ?' He showed himself capable of grasping these subtle shades: he had a taste for difficulties in love. I remember that heavy drops of rain were splashing on the roadway. At my request, Jean did not put on his mackintosh. I wanted a sodden appearance to increase still more his likeness to the youth who once had been heedless of the storms which it had been his mission to raise. On the stroke of five I pressed the door-bell. I felt terrified, and found myself counting the seconds of respite which I could still enjoy before the servant answered my summons. But Florence, no doubt, had been keeping her ears open, for the door was opened almost at once. I could see her, dressed in an outmoded linen frock, and trembling. Without saying a word she led us into the small drawing-room which a sudden break in the clouds had filled with the level light of the setting sun. She devoured Jean Queyries with her eyes, and he, silent and completely destitute of self-assurance, was darting his head this way and that like a young and terrified wild bird. My sister, in momentary uncertainty, passed her hand over her forehead. In the mortal silence of that pause, when I thought that I was attentive only to the thudding of my heart, I had sufficient detachment left to take notice, why I do not know, of the sound of a distant cab rattling on the cobble-stones at this late hour of a spring afternoon. At last Florence smiled. Her pale cheeks took on the colour of life, and an indescribable air of shyness, of modesty, imparted to this initiate of love, the virginal appearance, the swooning sweetness of a young fiancée. She made a sign that she could not speak, took his face between her hands, and gazed at him. With this living model before her, she was, no doubt, retouching the somewhat faded image of Augustin which she carried in her heart. She seemed scarcely at all surprised, already inured to the miracle, accepting, as perfectly natural, that the years should have left that dear face untouched—while I, sure now of my victory, was thinking only how I might exploit it. Meanwhile, the cab had stopped at the house. I was conscious of a shock when I heard the front-door shut. I knew that the servant had been told on no account to admit anybody. Steps sounded in the hall: there was a murmur of voices, and almost at once Madame Etinger, swathed in crape, entered the room.

'I would have you know, madame, that your insolent lackey actually tried to prevent me from having access to you!'

Florence smiled at her, and then, in a breathless voice, said: 'He is here!'

'Of course he is here, madame. Did I not promise to bring him?'

Before either of us could make a move she opened the door which she had closed behind her, and called to someone on the further side:

'Augustin!'

My hands were burning hot, and I pressed them to the marble top of the chimneypiece. A man came into the room. He was bald, and his face was like the faces of those who have passed through the furnace of atrocious climates. Though the whites of his eyes were yellow, though his lips were white, though there were two bitter folds at the corners of his mouth, and wave-like wrinkles on his forehead, I recognized him at once. Nothing was left of the old Augustin but the expression of his eyes. Everything else had been destroyed, but that had escaped from the ravages of time. He was neatly dressed in a new suit. He spoke:

'You have need of me? Here I am. You were right in believing that I have remained faithful. . . .'

I was overwhelmed with terror as one might be who has heard a dead man talk. Florence stared at him with a wild look in her eyes, Jean Queyries, a past-master at concealing his feelings, was in the embrasure of the window waiting for me to tell him what to do. Fortunately, Madame Etinger, unobservant but voluble, started to tell us of her journey. It had occurred to her that the simplest way of discovering Augustin's whereabouts—and it was extraordinary, she said, that I had not thought of it, too—was to get his address from the Trappist House in which our friend's father had died. But the presence of Jean Queyries seemed to trouble her. Discreetly, and with a conspiratorial air, she tip-toed to the door, making a sign to me to follow her, bringing the embarrassing intruder with me. When she had left the room, I was informed by Augustin that he had taken a job with a shipowner in one of the Western ports, and was due, very soon, to start for Dakar. Then he said:

'My friend! my old friend! . . .'

I realized that he dared not speak to Florence who was still completely tongue-tied.

'Ten years! how time does fly!'

This he followed up with all the routine things that are said when two old cronies meet again after a long separation which the deposits of many years have covered, making long familiar faces unrecognizable and strange. I had a foreboding that the once great spirit was in decline, was more hopelessly shattered even than his body.

All this while I was keeping a watchful eye on Florence. Her face was a stiff mask, expressing nothing. Suddenly she said:

'Make that man go away!'

Jean Queyries thought that the horrible words were meant for him, and with flaming cheeks made as though to leave the room. But she stopped him with a look of tender reproach:

'Where are you going, Augustin? Stay where you are.'

He halted. Clearly he did not know what to do, and looked a question. I made a sign that he should fall in with this mad mood of hers. She had turned to me, and now said, with the sulky look of an obstinate child:

'What is he doing here?'

For a brief moment Augustin looked at her with contempt in his eyes, and that imperious air which I once had known so well. But almost immediately his expression changed. A sudden lassitude, as though the whole man were drained and empty showed only too clearly that his inner powers of resistance had been for ever destroyed. There he stood, like a very poor, very old man. He was little more than skin and bone, but there was strength still in the structure of his face. But the sources of his life seemed to have dried up. What I saw before me was a beaten man, already touched by the huge indifference of death, so wholly abandoned that no denial could any longer surprise him. I put a finger to my head that he might think Florence mentally unbalanced, and led him away. In the hall he wrapped himself in a cloak of some coarse material. I stammered out a confused jumble of excuses, laying the blame for everything on my sister's incurable neuraesthenic condition. He seemed wholly apathetic and merely said: 'I understand . . . I am sorry my visit has not had the effect you hoped. . . .'

But on the stairs, where the flickering gas-flame merged

our two shadows, he began to dream aloud, as those who live alone so often do:

'Florence'—he said: 'was a young girl with a slim, sinewy body: what has this faded, heavy woman with the fleshy jowl to do with her? I remember that *my* Florence had a long neck with something of the pouter-pigeon about it. . . .'

In this way did he talk, and I, whom, at school, he had chosen for his friend, only once caught his eyes fixed on me, and then he turned them away immediately.

I could not help laughing: this meeting had been as disappointing for him as it had been for me. Each for the other was a ghost, and each had loved only an ephemeral grace, the spring-time of an hour, that one moment of time when every living being is a god: oh, youth so quickly gone!

We walked along the crowded quays, constantly separated by the flow of pedestrians. The din of trams and lorries drowned our voices, and, in any case, he spoke indistinctly, having lost his teeth. I remember him telling me the names of several African diseases. He spoke, too, of the murderous climate, of a cyclone which had destroyed his little settlement, and how physical weakness had made it impossible to rebuild it. Of the war he said nothing, except to describe the death-agony of a comrade who had had his shoulder torn away by a grenade when standing beside him. Meanwhile, with lifted head and half-closed eyes I saw again the verandah at Gravette, the white-crested waves merging with the heavy clouds, and Augustin with the wind in his hair. As we were passing a church, he made the gesture of taking off a non-existent hat. I caught the glance he gave to the shut door, and saw for a brief second a flicker of that flame which once had brought me happiness as well as a feeling of remorse. But it soon died out.

But it must have been smouldering under the ashes of the years to leap up suddenly like that merely at the sight of a drowsing church at a street-corner in the evening light. There came into my mind, just then, the dogma—of all articles of faith the most mysterious—of the resurrection of the body, and, for a moment I believed it, clung to it in a passion of hope. Could the wastage of the years resist Eternity? Will not all faces find again in God the splendour of their youth?—will not every heart be given back the power to love? Thus, as in the past, did Augustin free me, for a brief space, from the abyss into which I had fallen. From some obscure depth within myself his presence forced a groan.

He had taken a furnished room opposite the station. To reach it he picked so strange a route, that, at first, it seemed to me that he had lost his way. Then I realized that he was choosing the streets down which, returning from some expedition, we used to drag our weary feet. Time, which had ravaged our faces, had left the town untouched. The same shop-windows, so familiar to the eyes of childhood, still shone on the same pavements: and the smell was as it had been, a mingled smell of brine and mist. Between the banked roof-tops, the same river of sky still showed. In the crowd that thronged the narrow rue Sainte-Mathurine I found again that old remembered hour when the daylight dies more slowly, struggling against the glitter of the shops. In this confusion of electricity and dusk the warm wet wind had told the schoolboy, dawdling past the walls and talking to himself, of the good days to come. In the Cours Dauphine, a mob of idlers forced us to slow down. Augustin led me into the middle of the roadway. Dizzy with fatigue, I watched the pavement slipping by like a shore from which men saw our two bodies tossed upon the sea of time, or, rather, making an immense effort to swim against the irresistible current. We walked along the rue Judaique. Now and then, from the far end of an alley, a lantern cast a patch of colour on the entry to some furtive passage-way. The street thrusts into the darkness of the outer boulevards. Beyond it, in a cold blackness, the suburb, at that hour, was sleeping, with the probing evening light kindling the dirty windows to flame. No doubt Augustin did not want this nightmare walk to bring us to the palisade within which there lay our now dead spring, for he threaded his way along the boulevard in the direction of the docks. Gas-light eddying in the breeze lit up a drunkard's staggering steps. Between the motionless hulls of ships the reflections of the mooring lights trembled like the incandescent pillars of some upside-down palace. Tarpaulins sheltered piles of merchandise, and serried walls of pit-props made a strange city with streets smelling of resin. I remember that, at this point in our progress, Augustin told me something of his life in Paris, when he had come back for the first time from Africa. In a furnished room in the rue Berthollet he had rediscovered poetry. He bought at a baker's and a cold-meat shop just enough food to keep him from starving, and stayed out so long that the concierge thought he must be at a restaurant. He seemed to enjoy describing to me those methodical and rhythmic wanderings through the darkness. It was as though he were speaking, not of his own work, but of someone else's. A little further on, I ventured to ask him about his father's last moments. We had reached the darkest part of the docks, and he began to walk more slowly. I was careful not to look at the friend whose voice was the very same as that which had held Florence and me in an unending state of enchantment when, on the melancholy beach, we had heard it telling us the story of his life. He said that his father's death-pangs (according to those who had administered the last rites) had been terrible, but that the increase in his sufferings had brought joy to the dying man, because he did not doubt that one moment of agony could count for much in the saving of mankind at that dark hour of the war. Augustin spoke of the doctrine which sets an infinite value upon suffering, as though he, too, believed it.

'Perhaps,' he said, 'lives which, by the standards of this world, have been a failure, will, by those of the absolute, show as the only true successes.'

Was he speaking for himself or for me? We walked along the quays as far as the cross-roads where the bridge, loaded with lorries and trams, shows a double line of flame upon the water. We climbed down and went in under the enormous arch where sleeping bodies lay, and stood there for a long time without speaking, listening to the sound of the river making towards the sea. It was there, in the darkness, that we parted. Neither of us wanted to take a last look at the other's face. I even felt a strange eagerness to be alone, so that I might convince myself that this poor, unhappy man had not destroyed in me the image of the young Augustin. I loved his memory more than I loved him! No doubt this feeling was confused and unavowed. To see it for what it was, I had to come, by chance, last night upon that passage in Chateaubriand which is, surely, the cruellest confession ever made by a dying man: 'To part from actual things is nothing, but, from our memories, how different! For the heart breaks when it is torn from its dreams, so small a part does reality play in the consciousness of men.'

X

UGUSTIN's transit left me for several days in a prolonged brooding fit. I spent the time at home, dreaming and smoking. The tiller had slipped from my grasp, and I did not care. On the occasions of my rare visits to Florence it seemed to me that Jean Queyries was playing his part to perfection. I did not particularly want to know how her share in the duologue was shaping, and let myself be bogged down in a mood of security which had no real basis. After all, had not Hourtinat been swept out of our lives in precisely the way I had wished? But Florence's condition of inertia, the passive attitude of entreaty which seemed to be drawing the whole of herself upward toward Jean who, for his part, remained ensconced behind a barricade, one part of suspicion, one part of respect, should have put me on my guard. But it had needed no more than the ghost of Augustin to hold me tight in the rising tide of days long vanished. The past had become for me a powerful opiate. Happy are those who are blessed with the gift of a happy forgetfulness, who can use the scraps of their former lives as material with which to build up an everyday existence. Men of my type are obsessed by the gloomy pleasure of kneeling in adoration before what in them has been long dead. They are weighed down with memories, by visual recollections, by hoarded sensations, which, more than anything else, resemble corpses imperfectly embalmed. Somewhere deep within them the waters of the past stagnate and smell. I did not notice that Florence's home, like a ship about to founder, was deserted. Eliane was away with Madame Etinger, taking the waters at Salies, and my brother-in-law was no longer to be seen beside the domestic hearth. His valet had turned up one morning to fetch his suits and linen.

Everything should have served to warn me of this universal movement of abandonment, if only the instinct which kept me from the club, or, when I had to pass it, prompted me to avert my eyes from its door, since it was in the vestibule—as in the shop of a provision-merchant the finest of his stock is displayed in the window—that the smartest of the Sons, seated on the wicker sofa, showed to the public as from behind a pane of glass, the fine flower of their species. I am quite sure that, as soon as my approach was reported, they nudged one another, this being their way of passing the word that no notice was to be taken of my greetings. I had so frequently joined with them in inflicting this form of martyrdom on others! They quite literally don't see one. One lifts one's hat, one smiles, one waves a good-morning, but all in vain. They look at the sky, they gaze into a shop-window. It is as though one had upon one's finger the magic ring of invisibility. One almost doubts one's own existence. I have developed that flair, so strong in those who live in our town, for sensing insult from afar. With me it has become a second nature. Shortsightedness, and that trick I have of not being able to think clearly except when I am walking, insulate me from the street, and I move alone through even the densest crowd. Since seeing Augustin again I had become dug into that natural tendency. I no longer troubled to put up a defence. Faces deliberately turned away, hats tipped forward over foreheads—the whole plot hatched by Percy Larousselle missed fire completely thanks to my sudden insensitiveness, to that ability I had of being elsewhere, of escaping from the present. I took to avoiding the more crowded streets. To reach Florence's house I had only to cross the Public Gardens. On the quays, where I live, it is easy for me, by threading my way between the piles of barrels, to reach the far end to which none of the Sons would dare to penetrate.

One evening early in May, at the hour when gathering dusk empties the Gardens, I went there, meaning to settle down with a book. But it remained unopened, and, instead of reading I wandered in the warm and scented air and the half-light which I associated with the melancholy moods of boyhood, and with the faces I had known, now dimmed by time. In this lovely spot, at this season and this hour, it seemed to me that the young Augustin was once more as real and living as he had been before the irruption into my life of the poor and ageing creature who called himself Augustin. The contours of that jumbled image took on for me a new clarity, like those of a picture when it has been cleaned. A great calmness had descended on my heart. Cockchafers were on the wing. The tall, gilded railings separated me from the world of clanging trams. The magnolias glittered as though each leaf had been carefully tended on the lawns made more green and lustrous by the sprinklers' artificial showers. I was just savouring the refuge offered by these gardens, this dusk, this dark, dense curtain of new leaves, when a voice spoke my name. I turned my head and saw Florence. Her hat was perched crookedly upon her head: in her haste she had put on a light overcoat over an indoor dress.

'I was on my way to see you: there is something we have got to talk about.'

Florence scarcely ever climbed my stairs. It was a rule established once and for all between us that she should not. I realized that here was an end to the peace of mind which had become my place of safety since Augustin had vanished for the second time. Florence led the way, almost running, and I followed. The mist which for so long had lain between me and reality, now suddenly dispersed, and I was back in my customary state of mind, had become once more a young man living in a specific town and belonging to a definite social group. Tired and out of breath, Florence slowly climbed the stairs. The briefest of glances was enough to tell me that the battle was going badly. She sat down, and, when I switched on the light, complained that it hurt her eyes. I extinguished the lamps, and all the darkened room contained were two silent, shadowy figures. Swifts were uttering shrill cries above the river.

'Telephone to him, please: please telephone. He has given up coming: it is a whole week since I saw him last, and he doesn't answer my letters.'

I did not dare to ask who the faithless one was: did she mean Jean or Augustin?

'Bring him back if you value my life!'

I cannot reconstruct, not even for myself, Florence's monologue, her horrible confession, without feeling guilty. From what she told me, between fits of sobbing, I managed to get a pretty good idea of how the drama had developed during the time when, withdrawing from the fight, I had lost myself in brooding. From the very first, Jean had scrupulously stuck to his part. But what about Florence? At the moment when she had denied Augustin, she may have succeeded, very briefly, in cheating herself. After all, that denial could not possibly have been premeditated. Without reflection, without comparing and correcting, she had made her decision between the two men, had picked immediately the one her body had already chosen. Like all women who lack the saving grace which only spiritual love can give, she had surrendered to the exigencies of the flesh. But there could be little doubt that, once the wrong step had been taken, she had come to herself and realized with perfect lucidity what had happened. I understood from what she told me that not for a single moment during the ensuing days, had she been able to create for herself, so far as Jean Queyries was concerned, anything like a convincing illusion. I remember her very words, there, in the darkness of that room where she was sitting in a state of complete exhaustion:

'How could it have been otherwise? I had no time in which to get my bearings. Do you remember the wonderful plans we made for starting again, for achieving perfection? Well, in the space of a single second, they just collapsed in ruins at my feet. . . .'

'The fault was mine, Florence.'

But she told me to have no feelings of guilt.

'Do you really believe that if the other had come alone, if there had been no one else, I should have followed him?'

I understood then that she could not, would not, hold it against me that I had brought Jean into her life. Where is the woman who would prefer not to have loved—or who regrets having been loved? That is why Florence forgave my lie. And all this while she went on talking, endlessly. I sat down beside her, finding it difficult to catch what she was saying, and so it was that I came to realize the full horror of what my intriguing had set in movement. From that moment Florence had had eyes for nothing and nobody but that unknown young man who, so she had assumed, must be in love with her, since he had consented to play the part of lover. That was why she could not understand why it was that he resisted, why he did not, as she had done, throw aside the mask. Every day

Jean had paid her a long, respectful visit. The condition of complete abandonment in which she had been left made meetings easy in a house where no 'society people' would any longer show themselves. It was some time before Jean realized that she was stricken with the plague. If ever he had felt any genuine desire for her, now that he had only to lift a finger, the gigolo held back. He was thinking only of his own advancement, of how he would sneak his way into the empyrean of the Sons. The weaker her resistance became, the more did the horrid little cad assume towards her an attitude of veneration, and play with careful cunning the part assigned to him. Had he grown tired at last of waiting for the introductions that never came to the Percy Larousselles, the James Castaingts, the Willy Durands, the John Martineaus, the Bertie Dupont-Gunthers? Florence was for ever impressing on him the need to keep their 'affair' a secret: but he plumed himself on a show of innocence for which she felt no gratitude. In this way they had lived for many weeks, and all because of a misunderstanding. But, at long last, the moment came when it began to dawn on Jean Queyries that she was living in a solitude, an abandonment which, to say the least, was unusual. He had imagined that between himself and Madame Harry Maucoudinat there would be a deep and wide social gulf; that if he were to conquer this princess he would first have to force his way through many magic spells. But he had reached her without the slightest difficulty: all he had had to cross was a desert. The progress of his romantic story was proving too easy, too little hampered by vicissitudes, and in a silence which was like that of the end of a world. He scented disaster, became less punctual at their agreed meetings. Already he had set on foot a number of methodical enquiries. Since he was employed in our business, those experienced in the ways of the world were extremely reserved when he questioned them. Without contacts he might long have remained in ignorance. But the ill-luck which dogged us took him one evening to the *Lion rouge* where he found himself not far from the table at which Percy Larousselle, already pretty well liquored up, was telling one of his boon companions the story of our shipwreck. Jean Queyries, beside himself with fury, made no bones next day about reporting to Florence, pretty crudely, the horrible words which had reached his ears. How broken was the voice in which Florence described that final interview!

'I said to him—"what does all that silly tittle-tattle matter my dear? What does the world matter, so long as we love one another? What do we have in common with the world?"— These simple words were enough to show me the true nature of that little horror. I won't repeat the things he said to me. He was, himself, so deeply ashamed of them that he begged my pardon when he went away. But he did not come back, *that* is the disaster. Nothing else matters—he did not come back.'

She was crying now: her body was shaken with long-drawn sobs. There, in the darkness, that quivering figure filled me with feelings of horror and pity. I could do nothing but put my arm round her shoulders and wipe the tears from her face. I switched on the lights so that she might tidy her hair in front of the glass. Just as she was adjusting the veil over her eyes, my servant came into the room with a silver salver on which lay the evening post—some printed matter and several letters. At these she looked vaguely, and then, suddenly, with pointed finger, cried:

'There's a letter from him!'

Among ten samples of handwriting she had at once picked out Jean's, and, before I could stop her, had torn the envelope open. In a perfectly dead voice she read aloud the few lines in which the young man informed me that, owing to the slump in wines, he had decided to give up his present employment, and was going to travel for a big industrialist. Everything, he said, had been arranged at such short notice that he would almost certainly have to leave without saying good-bye to me.

Florence dropped the letter. She was no longer crying. I put her coat round her shoulders. She followed me without a protest. I hoped that we might avoid being seen by going through the Public Gardens, but the gates were closed upon the trees, now freed of humans, upon the inaccessible lawns. We had to walk along the pavement, exposed to humiliating meetings. Florence held her head high, and there was something terrifying in her smile. Perhaps, cost what it might, I should have forced her to shed tears. But I dared not take that risk with so many people about. Thanks to her state of apathy, she did not notice, at the corner of the Cours Dauphine, Percy Larousselle, with his bowler hat pulled down to his ears, and another of the Sons. We brushed against them, and I heard them laugh. Further on, Hourtinat dropped the arm of a tart who was with him, and seemed about to follow us; but his companion held him back. Like hunted animals, we almost ran, keeping close to the walls. I looked at nobody, but took refuge in my shortsightedness. At last we reached Florence's house. I had hoped that, in the small drawing-room where she had sat so often with Jean Queyries, she might give way to her grief. But scarcely had the door been opened to us than something mysterious in the expression of Florence's maid, warned me of disasters still to come. She told us that Monsieur had come in Madame's absence, had called for a set of tools, had forced open Madame's desk and had gone away with his despatch-case stuffed with letters. Florence was completely unmoved.

She did not seem to grasp what had happened. I took her into the small drawing-room, and showed her the open desk and the rummaged drawers. But she only shook her head and smiled.

'But, Florence'—I exclaimed—'don't you see that Harry has stolen enough evidence to get him a divorce twenty times over!'

She looked at me with a dazed expression and all she said was:

'There is something I don't understand . . . I will ask Jean to explain . . . You must go away now: he will be here in a moment, this is his regular time.'

She passed a hand over her forehead, over her eyes, still with that gesture of denial and that terrifying look. I rang and asked for some food to be brought her. The maid told us that no dinner had been prepared. The cook had given her notice to Monsieur, and he had paid her her wages. The only thing in the house was some cold meat which Florence ate with a good appetite. She was quite calm, almost gay, mysteriously protected against the harsh realities of life. She went to bed and to sleep, and the dreams she had were certainly not nightmares. A well-loved name died away on her lips. About two in the morning she opened her eyes, spoke the name once more, and then went back to sleep.

All this while I watched beside her. I, too, was calm. . . . I knew that in spite of the years, we had recognized you, Augustin, and that, from now on not time, nor absence, nor death itself, would ever free us of your presence.

XI

June, 19 . . .

IN this fisherman's hut, between the harbour and the ocean, I have gone to ground like a sick animal. I am hiding my nakedness. Bare, whitewashed walls, a sterile beach on which there is nothing but empty oyster-shells, sandy sea-wrack and dead jellyfish, an empty sky where, when the sun goes down, only a few clouds move apart, and, at times, the smoke of an invisible transatlantic liner—everything here combines to teach me the lesson of destitution. I am remaking myself in the image of this arid universe. Often I lie naked on the sands, or under the pines which seem so unreal that they give no shade. They hedge my body in, living torches of resin which, at times, under the August sun, go up in flames together.

Partial disaster would have left in me some relics of my earlier dwelling which I might have been tempted to use for the building of a new house. But of my former life nothing now remains but ashes. The pack of Sons has lost my scent, though there are days still when I can hear their baying. I have attained to a mood of complete tranquillity. I have few letters other than those from Florence, the tension of whose nerves is relaxing in the quiet existence of a nursing-home set in the peaceful green of growing things. I have never had from my sister such temperate pages, though sometimes a word reaches back so far that it is no wonder she still makes the psychiatrists uneasy. Stripped of everything, she delights in the thought of a future spent with me in this desert, where, together, we may seek access to the world of sanctity. It seems that now, for her who once was so fond of exploring the tangled ways of physical love, there is no longer any reality except within herself. A spiritualist woman friend is initiating her into the mysteries of the occult. I have no objection. She will learn, soon enough, that there is not one of our acts but will live on in us and possess us wholly. Satiety, disgust, the desire for renewal, all these states of mind are born of states more ancient. But I do not warn her against this. The important thing is that, in this lull, she shall gather strength to face the tempests still to come.

Harry Maucoudinat has good manners. Since his wife has been shut away he has discontinued his divorce proceedings. Madame Etinger is running his house and guiding Eliane's steps towards the heights. In a letter reeking of virtuous distress she has informed me that the attentions of Maître Balisac have strained her daughter's patience to the breaking point, and that, from now on, that chaste young woman will never live far from her mother. That is why she now adorns the Maucoudinat house. Knowledgeable in the art of mixing cocktails, she attracts the Sons there, and sings to them in a shrill music-hall voice songs with a tart flavour. An anonymous letter brings me the news that Madame Etinger is more favourably disposed to Harry than formerly, and no longer refers to him as either a chauffeur or an ostler. She maintains, on the contrary, that he is a 'child of nature' and likes to compare him to an 'element'. One evening, when there had been champagne, she had gone so far as to praise Percy Larousselle in whom, according to her, are to be found combined 'the refinements of an exquisite culture with the shamelessness of Primitive Man.' If I am to believe the writer of this letter (who must, I think, be Harry's mistress as she seems to be worried by all this

intriguing and anxious to enlist me on her side) Madame
Etinger is busy tacking, seeking the easier prey, not wishing to
betray us, and drawn, on the whole, to Percy who is a bachelor
with a pretty sharp nose for traps. It is, however, made clear
that there is no urgent need for my intervention. The Sons,
seated in a circle round Eva, keep a watchful eye on one another: as soon as any of them breaks the ranks a general
muttering forces him to retreat, and the whole pack gives
voice. No single man would dare defy those menacing throats.
How frightful is the fate of all young women! Eva, whose
warm lap the child Augustin loved so dearly; Eva, whose lips
could never touch the forehead of that wonderful boy through
the tangle of rebellious hair, men are now devouring with
their lidless, bloodshot eyes. Those monstrous, bald, arthritic,
overfed representatives of the rich middle-class, those car-
nivorous beasts of prey, are now using the tiny quantity of
imagination bestowed on them, in taking off her clothes in
thought, and, in fancy, using her body according to the rites
that most delight them . . . !

If I brood over all this baseness, the reason is that it interests
me to see how I react. It leaves me quite unmoved, and this,
at first, I found reassuring. But should I feel so calm had I not
been told that there is no real danger at home? Besides, since
Florence is shut away, nothing could better guarantee my
security for the moment. Under the pretext of turning over a
new leaf in solitude, it may be that, instinctively, I am following
the example of the ostrich and burying my head in the sand,
which is certainly the best way I know of dodging problems.
. . . But I try not to believe a word of this. No unworthy
motive keeps me here: I am concerned only for the welfare
of my soul, or so I try to persuade myself.

Often my wanderings take me to the place which, of all

others, is best suited to an examination of my conscience—
the inn where Augustin once sat between Florence and me,
and told us the story of his life. A trellis of leaves still rustles
in a wind from the sea. I no longer remember whether it was
on this table, or on that one further to the left, that we leaned
our elbows. The gramophone and the billiard-balls still make
more noise than the breaking of the short sea waves. As I grow
older, I imagine that no scene could mean more to me, because
of the eyes in which it was once reflected. Nothing draws me
to those savage lands on which the gaze, now dimmed in
death, had never rested in those days. Similarly, no newer
music can enchant me like the music I used to hear in those
lovely concerts of an older day, when I sat with his hand
in mine. How exigent the heart which draws all things to
itself!

I have just had a telegram saying that Florence has been
discharged and will be here tomorrow. They wouldn't have
let her go unless she were cured. This news ought to fill me
with great joy, but I do not feel it sufficiently. Am I displeased
to think that Florence is coming back into circulation? Has
all my sense of safety sprung from the knowledge that my
sister was shut away? Scarcely had I scrambled to my feet than
down I go again!

But in spite of myself I will be happy. This coming back must,
and shall, enchant me. There are upon this shore *immortelles*
and sea-pinks which I can use to decorate her poor little room.

August, 19 . . .

From my window I can see, down there upon the shore,
lying beside Florence who is sunning herself, another slimmer
figure—Miss T . . . , the friend she made in the nursing-home

where both were cured. Florence deliberately leaves upon my
table books which treat of the occult sciences. Miss T . . . is
persuading her to live among the dead. Nevertheless, it is the
same Florence who has been restored to me, with a face
scarcely more worn, but softer now, drowsy, and as though
carrying a load of dormant passions. All the ardour which she
used in her search for love is now wholly absorbed in colloquies
and supplications designed to keep an invisible interlocutor
chained to a table or planchette. I, myself, am so hostile to these
practices that, according to Miss T . . . my mere presence is
enough to frighten the spirits away. This thin little sandy-
haired creature, with sickly eyelids fluttering in a freckled
face, would like me to take myself off. How happy it would
make her to throw me back into that world in which I feel—
with what an overwhelming sense of self-disgust—it might be
rather pleasant to set foot again! But am I to leave my sister
to the mercies of this female necromancer? Florence preaches
her new faith to me, and is amazed that I should be repelled
by it. How can I convince one so deep in dreams that not by
her road shall I manage to escape from myself? In all the
unmapped sky is there no other gate by which I may enter?
Following in Augustin's footsteps I have hung about the
presbytery where lives a sturdy great curé who is out to catch
not men but fish, and grumbles if he is got out of his bed to
carry consolation to a dying man. I had much hope of a young
priest who has come here to nurse his one remaining lung,
because he has the face of a martyr and eyes that blaze more
intensely than those of the abbé Lacordaire in Chassériau's
portrait. But no sooner had I taken him into my confidence
than he advised me to read again, in the *Ethics*, those theorems
in which Spinoza points out to us the way of joy. If the salt
hath lost its savour wherewith shall it be salted? In what

country parish, in what cell, dwells now the suffering saint who will lead me to salvation? You only, Augustin, were for me the incorruptible salt. Till now it has been in you alone that I have tasted it, and I cannot live without the memory of that bitter savour on my lips.

THE END